Mondays Are Red

Mondays Are Red

NICOLA MORGAN

Delacorte Press

Published by
Delacorte Press
an imprint of
Random House Children's Books
a division of Random House, Inc.
New York

Visit us on the Web! www.randomhouse.com/teens
Educators and librarians, for a variety of teaching tools, visit us at
www.randomhouse.com/teachers

Library of Congress Cataloging-in-Publication Data

Morgan, Nicola.
    Mondays are red / Nicola Morgan.
        p.   cm.
Summary: When he wakes up from a coma after having meningitis, fourteen-year-old Luke finds that he has lost control of his senses and his thoughts and he must fight an inner demon in order to return to his former life.
    ISBN 0-385-73099-3 (trade)—ISBN 0-385-90128-3 (GLB)
    [1. Sick—Fiction.   2. Synesthesia—Fiction.
    3. Brothers and sisters—Fiction.]   I. Title.
    PZ7.M82615Mo   2003
    [Fic]

                                                    2003003651

The text of this book is set in 12-point Goudy.

Printed in the United States of America
October 2003
10 9 8 7 6 5 4 3 2 1
BVG

Mondays Are Red

A Kaleidoscope in
My Head

Mondays are red. Sadness has an empty blue smell. And music can taste of anything from banana purée to bat's pee. That's what I need to explain, starting with the day it all began, the day I woke up in a hospital bed with a kaleidoscope in my head. I discovered later that I had almost died from meningitis but I remember nothing about that bit. My first memory is the dizzy waking up part and my soggy muddled head. My second memory is how, bit by bit, I began to realize how much my world had changed.

A volcano spat me furiously with a roar from its mouth. Bagpipes whined in my ears as I shot head over heels through the watery darkness, spinning fizzy. Away from the purple pain, too fast to breathe, blood cartwheeling in my veins. Floating somewhere, anywhere, until suddenly with a magnesium flash I was lying white on a bed and I knew immediately that I was in a hospital. How cool! How dramatic!

I struggled to focus on the people around me. There was

Mum. A salty brightness in her smudged eyes. Dad was shouting for a doctor or a nurse or anyone.

"Come quick! Luke's awake!" And the girl with wasps in her straw-straight hair was Laura, my older sister. Two ugly years older. A perfect age for poisoning. If I had felt strong enough I'd have tied her by her hair to a chair and put a spider down her neck while a forest fire raged outside her prison hut. A huge soft spider with hunched-up sticky brown legs and deep alien eyes.

I felt odd. Floating. With weird words in my head and unnatural pictures behind my eyes. What was happening?

A yellowy doctor with weedy glasses spoke. Was that a weasel watching me carefully from behind his eyes?

"Hello, young man. Can you remember your name?"

"Rumpelstiltskin, stupid!" spat a cobra from my mouth. The doctor flinched and pinched the edges of his smile, a spasm jerking his blobby neck. "Luke!" gasped Mum.

"Well, I see we're on the mend, then!" He laughed as he made some notes on the chart in his hand. I could see Dad trying to read what it said. Laura was picking at a lilac fingernail.

My head throbbed black slime and I wished they all would go. But as Mum stroked my hand, strawberry music flowed from her fingers, softening my muscles. My vision went limp, spiraling into my head, and my eyes started to fog over.

What happened next was extraordinary. Even I knew that, drowsy as I was.

Have you ever done one of those magic-eye picture puzzles? Where you look at the pattern and force your eyes to relax, lose focus and go cross-eyed? If you succeed in this almost-impossible letting go, you suddenly see deep inside, behind, beyond the picture, and a whole new world appears. That's what happened to me.

It was then that I properly noticed the wasps in Laura's hair, at the same time as I realized that they shouldn't be there. They couldn't be there, but they were. They crawled around her face and into her nose. And around and about I could see rows of flowers of every possible shade of every imaginable color. Musical notes danced as they sang, each with a smell and a taste. Several brushed over my tongue like cobweb candy floss. I saw the tips of my fingers start to soften and swell, as weird insects fluttered out and lined up to the right. I could see every color, taste, smell, song, idea, possibility, feeling, wish. I could have whichever one I wanted.

It was as if a huge transparent computer screen had been put really close to my face. In fact, it was more like being *in* a computer and looking out, so that I was seeing first the things on the screen and in my head and then everything outside the computer, the real, other world beyond. Distantly, I could see the washing-up-liquid-green walls of my small room, the curtains with headachy corkscrew patterns, a bag of fluid dangling above me and a monitor with zigzag lines I didn't want to look at. This was all hazy through the screen, whereas everything *on* the screen was now sharply in focus.

In the top right corner of my vision sat the most extraordinary creature you could imagine, even if you had the most extraordinary imagination in the universe. Hunched and shapeless, it brooded, waving countless writhing arms. Acrid yellow steam rose from its armpits. Yet, when I looked more closely, curiously, it seemed to change somehow and I could see that its face was almost human. Long white hair, perfectly brushed, framed transparent skin, like clingfilm, wrapping a delicate spider's web of blue veins. As I stared, the creature turned its face toward me, its pupils paper-thin slits as it returned my mesmerized gaze. Its lips swelled into a smile. It was an orange-scented smile that seemed to flood my bloodstream with promises of pleasure. It was a smile that cast a spell.

"Go on. What are you going to do?" it said, without appearing to speak. The voice just oozed into my brain.

"Nothing," I said inside my head. I couldn't think of anything more interesting than that. I was completely transfixed. It was what I normally would have said; but inside me there were more jumbled thoughts and wordless feelings that I had never had before. In there, it felt like being on the dizziest, most beautiful-frightening roller-coaster ride ever invented. The sort where all you can do is lie back and scream and want it to end and yet want it never to end.

"You can't do nothing," the creature said. "Logically and philosophically, that would be impossible. To do nothing is a choice you make. It is, therefore, something. On another level, you can't do nothing because you mustn't do nothing. Doing nothing is, quite simply, my friend, a waste. A waste of what you now have."

His cleverness confused me. My head hurt. I wanted the ride to end.

I closed my eyes. The screen was still there. I squashed them tighter till blood cells shrank and squeezed their way through tiny vessels. Still the same screen, just more purple and more tightly dancing. I opened my eyes again.

"Who are you, anyway?" I asked.

"My name is Dreeg. I'm here to guide you."

"I don't need to be guided."

"Oh, I think you do. Things are very different now."

"Nothing's different. I've just been ill. I'll get better. Everything will be the same."

"What color are Mondays?" asked Dreeg.

"Red."

"There you are! I told you everything was different! What do you mean, 'Mondays are red'? Have you ever said that before? Taste this tune." One of his arm-things snaked out and he picked up a flower. I heard a lemony bitterness wail from a violin and tears swelled up from the deepest deep-down part of me.

"Stop! Turn it off!" I shouted. Because I knew what he meant. Mondays had never been red before. Mondays had had no color at all before. Mondays were simply days that followed Sundays and meant no PE at school. But now when I thought of Monday, I saw red velvet, felt its warmth, tasted the corners of its softness. And I knew that violin music would not have sounded like lemons or made me cry the day before I fell ill.

I looked at Laura through the screen now. Before my eyes, as I watched, her mouth became a glistening slick-brown slug. This was how I saw her. A slug eating strawberries. A wood louse curled itself up cringing in the pit of my stomach. It smelt of unnatural hate.

What was happening to me? Why, when I saw things

through the screen, did I see them in forms that could not be real, and yet that felt more real, more true than anything else? It was dizzying, overwhelming, and yet felt as brilliant as screaming. I wanted the ride never to end.

There was something else. A memory, sharp and green, suffocating. It seemed to come from a thick gas that seeped from Dreeg's fingertips. A memory thrashing about in my head. What was it? I tried to snatch it and form it into a thought sentence but as soon as I tried, it dispersed like squid ink. All I knew was that it felt important.

Ugly, too. I didn't want to think about it or look any longer at Laura's mollusk face. With a huge effort, I sent the thought message PISS OFF! through my head. The screen melted away and the normal world was clear again. If I looked hard I could still see Dreeg like a little icon in the corner. I decided to ignore him. Perhaps he would go away completely. His presence was too strange for comfort.

I looked at the faces around my bed. No one was looking at me oddly. I must not have spoken aloud. Whatever it was, was all happening in my head. Not real.

Laura was becoming restless. I could see that she probably wanted to say something like "I'm glad you're getting better, Luke," but she couldn't quite bring herself to do it. I was getting far more attention than she could bear. Something inside me grinned.

"Jon, why don't you take Laura and go and get something to eat?" said Mum. Off they went, Dad doing a thumbs-up sign at me as he left and Laura smiling at the doctor. Everyone always said she had a lovely smile.

"What a pleasant girl your Laura is," they would say to Mum and Dad. I saw it differently.

Mum stayed beside me and held my hand as though she couldn't let go. Mum is usually the calmest, most unworrying person you can imagine. Now she seemed taut, stretched. Without any makeup, she looked tired. I could tell but could not bear to think about what was in her head.

"What day is it?" I asked.

"Tuesday."

Orange. Pale apricot ice cream. I wanted the ride never to end.

"You've been in hospital since Friday. You've been asleep."

Friday. Melting chocolate oozing over my tongue.

"In a coma, you mean?"

Mum looked at the doctor. He took over. "Well, kind of, Luke, but then we kept you asleep for a while to let your body recover. You're going to be fine now. How are you feeling?"

"My head hurts. There's a beehive inside. I feel weird, weak. I feel like I've been drowned in sand. And my eyes are buzzing hot. Hummingbird-orange hot."

The doctor turned to Mum. "That's a clever lad you've got. Good with words."

"Tell his teachers," joked Mum, though with a hint of puzzlement. "Maybe being ill has done him some good."

The doctor turned to me. "You're going to be fine. You'll feel a bit under the weather, tired, for a while but before long you'll be just fine. And some time off school—expect you like the sound of that? In the morning, we'll run some tests and then—"

"What sort of tests?" asked Mum, echoing just what I'd been thinking.

"Oh, just routine for someone who's been ill like Luke. Reflexes, strength, things like that. Make sure everything's just as it was before."

There was a small gray cloud floating above our heads. Sitting on it, Dreeg winked at me. "Tomorrow," he chuckled. "Let's see—that will be Wednesday." He smiled.

Wednesdays are sweet light green with a brown tinge, like the apples my grandpa grows.

Dreeg's smile now was not the same one that had caught me in its spell before. It was the smile of someone who never loses. Already, there was something different about his appearance. I couldn't quite catch what it was. Perhaps his skin was tinged with yellow or the slits in his eyes were even narrower. Something cold wriggled down my back.

"I want to sleep," I said, shutting my eyes. As they left the room and Dreeg slumped into the corner of my brain, I knew that things were not going to be just as they had been before. Nothing was ever going to be the same again. I wanted the ride to end.

In the darkness of my insides, a tiny snake of strange fear hatched from its shell and flickered its tongue for the first time. Away it slithered under a stone and hid there. Waiting. For what, I didn't know and couldn't ever have imagined.

A Certain Weakness

When I woke next morning the room was white with summer. I remembered instantly where I was. As soon as I tried to move my arm, I felt the needle and saw the thin clear tube attaching me to a drip. A hollowness in my stomach reminded me that I had not eaten for days. Amid a background of voices, I could hear a distant clanking of metal and hoped that this would be breakfast. I needed some strength. As it was, it was all I could do to move my hand.

A clock high on the wall told me it was just after six. I grinned and stretched my feet as I realized that in other people's houses alarm clocks would soon be telling them to go to school. And I could just lie here and wait for my breakfast as the warmth of the sun lasered through the glass.

With a shock, I realized I would miss athletics training.

I needed to get back home, out of here. The summer term was the best time of year, when the days were long and the evenings elastic and the yellow air full of possibilities. I had to get home and then everything would be normal. Panic singed the edge of my brain. I remembered the fear that had flickered inside me the day before. It was the fear of change, of the unknown, of a new reality. I wanted everything to be normal. I had forgotten the thrill of the ride.

I looked quickly but I couldn't see Dreeg. Perhaps what had happened yesterday was some strange effect of my illness. Or a dream. And everything would be back to normal today.

A nurse came bustling into my room and tapped the bag of nameless liquid that snaked into my arm. "Hello, honeybun. Wonderful Wednesday morning." And off she went.

Wednesday. My grandpa's apple color, flooding my eyes from behind. The smell of green washed over me and I shivered. Yesterday had not been a dream.

Sure enough, Dreeg was there. I think he had been there all the time, a brooding presence in the far corner of my vision. He definitely did not look the same as yesterday. The differences were clear. His eyes were yellow and rheumy, with no pupils at all. On his face, the veins that had been gossamer-light were bulging in places, pulsing. His hair, now nicotine-tinged, was unbrushed, and too thin to hide his flaking scalp.

"Good morning, Luke," he said, grinning through his now beaky octopus-mouth, unfolding some of his arms to shift his position. "How did you sleep?"

"By closing my eyes and waiting," I replied inside my head. I felt somehow compelled to answer him, although I would rather have ignored him. He was a part of my thoughts.

"Hah! Very good! Very perceptive and accurate! One might even say, precise. And intelligent."

10

I said nothing. I couldn't decide if he meant to praise or if he was mocking me. He continued, "What color is Friday?"

"Don't be stupid. Days of the week don't have colors. Music doesn't have a taste. Thoughts don't have smells."

"Did I say that thoughts have smells, Luke? I don't believe I did. But you obviously think they do. What's so odd about the idea?"

"Normal people don't think like that. Normal people think—know, actually—that days of the week are just names, music is just sound and thoughts are just stuff in your head."

"People talk about the smell of fear, though. What is the smell of fear, Luke?"

"Smoke in a locked room, poisoned lipstick in a masked man's hand, and a bicycle rolling along with no rider." I don't know why I said all that. It just came out. I blushed. What was I? Weird, or what?

"Very good, Luke. Very creative now. Most significantly creative."

Forget creative. We had to do creative writing at school. Girls' stuff, sissy, with adjectives and daffodils and shimmering sunlight and feelings and stupid words like *metaphor*, just to describe other words. Dreeg was looking uglier by the minute, changing before my eyes. Oozing yellow pus from his mouth. Flies crawling into his nose.

Another nurse came into the room with normal good-morning-type chatter, stuck a thermometer in my mouth and put her fingers softly on my wrist while looking at the watch pinned to her cardigan. "Good, good, good," she said, and scribbled secret figures on my chart. "How are you feeling today?"

"Fine. Hungry. Bored."

"Hungry and bored means you're getting better. Let's get you sitting up." She competently pulled me upright, though I didn't need this help, and as her warm perfume sang me a dream, autumn leaves floated around her head and I felt chestnuts roasting on an apple-wood fire. OK, so I know I have never experienced chestnuts roasting on any fire at all, let alone an apple-wood one, but I am just saying what I felt.

"Do you like it?" asked Dreeg, after the nurse had gone.

"What?"

"Chestnuts roasting on a wood fire? And copper colors with the taste of autumn? Fireworks, toasted marshmallows, disguise and laughter? The smell of bracken and eating blackberries in the late sun?"

As he said each thing, I felt it throughout me. Really felt it. It was as though he was saying what was already in my head, speaking out my thoughts, my own words. I knew the ideas in every part of my body. Not just words but something real. It was embarrassingly fantastic.

"It's all right," I said grudgingly.

At the same time, I realized that Dreeg himself had now taken on an autumn glow. He stroked my brain, with fingers soft as meringue. His skin was apple-healthy. It seemed to me that his appearance changed depending on my own feelings about him. He was a chameleon, reflecting my thoughts.

"That's what I can show you," he said, puffing himself up. "You think words are nothing but pap. You think cool is only football and spiders down your sister's back. You think being creative is arty farty stuff for wimps or weirdos. I can show you that words are stronger than anything, that you can do anything with them. With my help," he added, licking his lips.

His face was a fanatic's, spitting consonants, all wild eyes and sweat. He talked crazy stuff. I turned away. "You're talking rubbish. I'm not into words." I pushed him into the corner of my brain, where he folded himself like plasticine into a splodge. I could sense him looking at me, as though disappointed, but I didn't know what he expected. I certainly wasn't interested in changing myself for him. Why should I?

Breakfast came. It was soggy but I was hungry. I ate it all. Afterward, a boring list of things was done to me, to my bed, to my chart. Groups of doctors came and stood around and smiled and muttered, wrapping themselves in words like armor. Mum and Dad came, not Laura. "Laura sends her love, Luke, but she's had to go to school."

Oh yeah! That must have been a tough decision—go to school or visit Luke. There was some boyfriend at school, sporting-hero type, all tan and gel and taut muscles and lazy voice and a swagger.

Swirling in the inkiness at the back of my brain, that memory shifted itself again. The taste of vomit. Something sluglike-sounding. It was gone before I could know it.

Later that morning came the tests. A group of white coats stood around my bed and smiled the taste of flour. Mum and Dad were still there, too, and I could see them try to merge into the background, awkwardly. I didn't like the feeling that they were not in charge. A deep frown creased Dad's forehead. I could tell he was worried. But then, he usually was. Dreeg shifted his seething mass in the corner and smiled secretively, as though he knew what was going to happen.

I don't quite know if I passed or failed these tests. They didn't seem very difficult. A doctor put my limbs in certain positions and tapped bits with a hammer. My knees jerked up as I knew they were meant to do—we did this on each other at school. He tapped the inside of my ankle and scratched the sole of my foot and I'm not quite sure what was meant to happen so I don't know if it did. I had to push against the doctor's hands in different directions and squeeze his fingers, and all with these people watching with their unknowable expressions.

Then came the moment when I had to get out of bed and stand up. Of course I was weak from being in bed for several days. Anyone would have been. The fact that I fell over—or would have done if two of them had not been quick enough to catch me—should not have been surprising for them or me. I don't know what their faces said because I was looking at the ground, but Dreeg was grinning. Almost jumping with excitement.

The worst part was that I knew why I fell over and it wasn't because I'd been in bed for so long. I fell because my left leg didn't work properly. It felt as though it wasn't there. I looked at it. It looked like fog. When I touched it, it felt normal and it could feel being touched, though a bit distantly. But it looked like fog and it didn't work.

Of course, I know it didn't really look like fog, not in the sense people usually use, in the real world. But to me it did, just as Laura's hair looked as though it had wasps in it and her lips looked like a slug eating strawberries. In my new way of seeing things, my leg looked like fog. It's the only way I can describe it. It felt like fog, so my brain made it look like fog.

Glancing at each other, the white coats made noises along the lines of "Hmmm, yes, some weakness there—some neurological impairment—put him down for physio—bring him back in a few weeks—must get some rest now—" Blah, blah, blah.

Some of the white coats wrote things down, and they all left the room without looking at me again. Mum smoothed my sheets and Dad asked if I wanted anything. He nervously made some joke about me being lucky having such pretty nurses. "Shut up, Dad," I snapped, and Mum almost said something but stopped herself. She put her hand on Dad's shoulder and he subsided.

"Tom asked if he could come. I said he could this afternoon," said Mum brightly through a seaweed mist.

That was the best news I'd heard. Tom had been my closest friend ever since I could remember. The sort of friend you could depend on to be on your side. Right or wrong. We were the best runners in our year. He might be a faster sprinter but he would never beat me at the 800 meters. No one could.

Mum and Dad left soon after and I spent the next hour trying not to think about my leg. It would get better. It must get better. Nothing else was possible. If there was something to worry about, the doctors would have told me, wouldn't they?

If this was Wednesday and Wednesday was athletics, would they be choosing the team today? The interschools competition was only about three weeks away. They couldn't leave me out. I might only miss today, that was one Wednesday and maybe one Friday, too. I would make it up, run harder, eat more, suck up to the teacher, go to church, kill someone, anything.

Dreeg puffed at a pipe like the caterpillar in *Alice in Wonderland*. He smelt of cold batter, late homework and a fat woman's sweat.

"Give it up, Luke. It's not worth worrying about. You can do much more interesting things with your life."

"Bog off. Leave me alone." My head fizzed.

"Now, now, no need to be so rude. You'll find I'm quite fun to be with, actually. And much more useful than you think."

"I can't imagine that."

"Oh, you will. You will." I didn't like this arrogance, this assumption that he could just invade my head and say anything he wanted. He was a wart and I wanted to be cured of him. Wanted my life back.

They came for me with a wheelchair later in the day. I slumped into it and tried to hide as I was wheeled down cold corridors toward the physio department. The porter couldn't tell I wasn't in the mood for his jokes. He thought being jolly was part of his job, I suppose. I wasn't interested in his job. I just wanted not to be there, stuffy indoors, when outside the sun would be scorching the grass and my friends would be laughing as they ran. And everyone else's lives were just the same as before.

I couldn't help this anger, this bitter voice of self-pity. My head hurt and everything stank.

I am ashamed to say that I cried during this first physio session. As I bit back the unfairness, I could see Dreeg in my head, sitting on a basketball net, a laughing maggot.

"Give it up, Luke. I can show you better things than this. I can show you how to create things, be like a god, make things happen."

I didn't know what he was on about, with his passion, bright boiling eyes and fancy talk about creating. Who wanted to be like a god? All I wanted was to walk like normal people. And run, jump, kick. Just as well as I had before.

"I will get better," I snarled at Dreeg on our way back to the ward.

"I don't really care that much whether you do or don't," he snapped. "It's not an either-or situation, you know. Besides, I've got more interesting things to show you."

"I don't have to look." But I knew I did. I even knew that I almost wanted to but I didn't know why. However much he might irritate me, he fascinated me and I wanted to listen to him. After all, he was in my head. I was, you could say, falling under his spell.

His voice was maple syrup on pancakes and his eyes drew me into their perfectly round centers. Pupils now like doughnuts.

Dreeg grinned.

As I came back along the corridor, I could see straight into my room. There was a figure by my bed. Tom. And a football. He turned at that moment and saw me. In a wheelchair. I saw it in his shocked face. And in the way he quickly shoved the football behind his back. It was raining in the room, steel shards of water.

Panic. I froze. I couldn't be seen by Tom like this. I was looking through that computer screen again. Dreeg was there, shouting at me from inside the tangle in my head. "Do something, Luke. Deal with it."

Insect with
Acid-Green Antennae

I hadn't the faintest idea what he meant. All I knew was that I wished I wasn't in a wheelchair, wished that Tom hadn't felt the need to shove the football behind his back. Was it so obvious that I wouldn't play again?

On the computer screen in front of my eyes the images danced around, teasing, and I couldn't catch them. Didn't know what to do.

Dreeg hissed, "Use your mind. Be creative. Get your head round the idea. Squeeze the want inside."

Sure enough, if I really concentrated, really looked inside and almost turned my brain inside out, I could grasp the images with my mind, as though I had an invisible mouse to control them with. One insect, with acid-green antennae, seemed to spring out of the screen. Some of the other pictures on the screen started to come together. Slowly, and then more quickly, a picture formed, and my mouth started speaking, almost without my control.

"Like my new speed machine? Check the ice-blue gleaming bodywork, cool alloy wheel trim, technobubble fiberglass dashboard. Feel the chill taste of power. The song of danger." The porter clearly wondered what had got into this previously dull lump. Tom looked equally perplexed. But, you know, the most amazing thing of all was that for a brief moment the wheelchair actually did look like a racing car. Then when I looked at it again, although my eyes could see that it was just a clanky heavy old hospital wheelchair, in my mind it was as I had described it. Tom and the porter were looking at the chair in amazement, too. "Cool!" said Tom.

I tried not to look at Dreeg, but I admit that he smelt of milk shake, soft and floury-thick on my tongue.

I managed to get myself into bed without looking too pathetic. "Don't really need that, you know. It's just the nurses want me to use it for today. 'Squite fun, though?" I grinned.

"Can I have a go?" asked Tom.

I didn't know what had happened, or how or why, but I knew that it didn't matter anymore about the wheelchair.

"No, you can't, young man. More than my job's worth. See you, Luke." Off went the porter with the chair, pirouetting down the corridor outside my room and making zooming noises through the sides of his teeth.

Tom wanted to know everything about my illness. There wasn't much I could tell him. I certainly didn't tell him about Mondays being red. He said they had had to pray for me in school assembly. I was a hero, apparently. No one had ever been prayed for in assembly and survived.

As we settled into our usual talk, normality began to feel

closer. The spike of Tom's hair stuck up at exactly the same angle as it always had. He fiddled with his mobile phone as he always did.

We didn't talk about athletics or sport at all. The football he had brought was nowhere to be seen. But I noticed on the floor the insect with acid-green antennae. Later, I found out why. And it changed everything. Completely.

Home three days later. All Saturdays are yellow but this June day was sticky with lemon honey. I thrust my hand out of the car window, resting the whole weight of my arm on the wind as Dad drove me the few miles home.

Our house sits on its own. We live near a village in Yorkshire, very close to the River Ouse. If I stand at my front door, I can see the village, and Tom's house. But if I stand at the back door, there are no houses to be seen. Fields and pinewoods surround us. The woods are full of silent mystery, with wide grassy tracks separating the sections of trees. At every junction are racks of broomsticks and buckets of sand, with DANGER OF FIRE! signs.

For me, my woods are space and escape. For Dad, whose job is with the forestry commission, they are a place of work. He doesn't see the wild mystery of them, only their dull statistics and unlikely dangers. Get him onto the subject and he can bore you rigid with the botanical facts about any tree species you can name. And in the summer, he can't walk through woods without stooping to pick up tinder-dry grass and rub it between his fingers. He frowns as he looks at the sky. "Hmm, not a rain cloud to be seen," he will say in a worried voice, his thick hair graying at the sides. Everyone else might plan a trip to the beach—but Dad will want to keep an eye on the woods.

Freedom floated through the car window and buttery flute music spread over my face.

My house. Everything the same. There was Laura in a tiny bikini on the sun lounger, talking on her pink mobile phone. Mouth like an unripe cherry, acid and tart. There was Mum coming to the door. And Amber, our dog, my dog, rushing out between Mum's legs with manic barks. I opened the car door and decided that my stick was going to get in the way so I just sort of tumbled onto the grass and was smothered by dog. Mum pulled Amber off and held her back as I lumbered to my feet and limped, leaning on my stick, into the house.

I had pretty much refused point-blank to take the wheelchair home. My leg needed to get stronger, I reasoned, and how could it do that if I sat in a chair all day? I may have pretended to Tom and the porter that it was a racing car but it was still, to be honest, a wheelchair. And I wasn't having it.

"Come on, Laura, Luke's home," called Mum.

"Got to go, Paul, my baby bro's home . . . yes, that one . . . no, worse luck." She made some cringe-making girly noises before switching the machine off and strumping into the house.

Later that evening, she went out. I saw her before she went and something crawled inside me, somewhere in the bit you breathe from. It shrank my airways. How could she dress like that? The makeup of a slag, tiny clothes, a stick-on tattoo of a devil on her shiny shoulder. Who was she trying to please? That green acid memory again, taunting me with the vapor of something horrible. And yet again it swirled away as soon as I tried to think it in words.

These thoughts left nettles in my mouth. As I looked at her, I realized something disturbing: that although I might not have particularly liked Laura before, this disgust, this physical feeling of hatred, was new. It was something that had started when I woke up in hospital, when I began seeing everything weirdly. Why did I hate her so much? What had changed?

Feeling like this seemed like a part of me. Just as Dreeg was part of me. But, just as I knew that Dreeg had not always been part of me, so I also realized that I had not always had these feelings about Laura. Some part of me knew that feeling this way was not normal. So what had happened? And why?

Before I could think further, without warning I was looking through the computer screen. Now Laura looked like the jerky victim in a video game, being pursued by a black metal man, faceless, with a mercury mask. Each time she turned round I could see her saucer-eyed panic. The man's mask was stretched in a grin as he threw a net made of sticky spiders' webs over her and she collapsed tangled in the gunge, the silly heel of her shoe broken among the ashes of a fire. The man started to melt into a metal snake, which coiled itself around her neck. Her eyes bulged as it started to tighten.

"Make sure Paul walks you back," called Dad, worrying again.

"Eleven-thirty. At the latest. Keep your phone on," called Mum. Mum not worrying again. Mum made arrangements so detailed and controlled that there was never anything left to worry about.

Something bad was going to happen to Laura one day. I could feel it. She would only have herself to blame, with the way she dressed and behaved. I tried not to think about whether I minded.

Whatever my reason, I lay awake that night and listened for her. It was way past eleven-thirty when I heard her giggling on the doorstep for several minutes, followed by the raised voices of the row she well deserved. Flitting unwelcome into my head came the sudden smell of that memory again. Surely the edges of it were clearer now? A gray wall. A green-gray wall, weakness and a sweet smell. Of pine. Disinfectant. That was it. Pine disinfectant. But what did it mean and why did it blow its spores into my face each time it passed through me? Why the shooting pain that clenched my head each time I tried to catch it?

The Circular Smell of an Apple

A **week off school,** but I don't remember much about the first two days. My head ached and I spent most of that time with my eyes shut and the curtains closed. Once I started to feel better I was bored. Tom was at school, Dad was at work, and Mum had taken time off but wasn't much help on the boredom front. Besides, she kept looking at me, as if she thought I might be ill again at any moment. It was something she couldn't plan against.

I thought at first that the weirdness in my head—the computer screen stuff—was just a temporary effect of being ill. But I soon began to see that it wasn't. As the actual symptoms of the illness quickly faded, the magic-eye world became stronger.

I was seeing the world through mixed-up senses. I was seeing music and smelling colors and tasting what my fingers told me. If I say "apple" to you, a picture of an apple comes into your head, as if in front of your eyes. But if you say "apple" to me, the apple is in me, with its colors traveling down my arms and a circular smell in my ears.

And if you want to know the weirdest bit—it's this. Although an apple to you can be certain shades of green or red, an apple to me has different colors in my head. It is white in the middle, because the letter *p* is white. And the letter *a* is minty green, while *l* and *e* are different shades of pink. So everything is more to me than it is to you. A kaleidoscopic shower. Beautiful and confusing.

I didn't know if anyone else was like this. But I didn't want to ask in case the answer was no. To be odd is to be mad and lonely, which are the most frightening things in the whole weird world.

With my physiotherapy exercises, my leg did become stronger, though not as quickly as I wanted. I could walk without my stick by Tuesday, though my limp was obvious. I did my exercises more often than I was supposed to, desperate to run as soon as possible.

The week, hot and limp, had just begun to drag.

But then, on Wednesday, something totally extraordinary happened. It showed me just how much everything had changed. Showed me temptation and pulled me in headfirst.

I flew.

I had just come back from physio and was already doing one of my exercises. This involved standing on my good leg and using the hazy leg to move a ball in a figure-eight pattern. It required concentration and I was tired. My head melted in the heat.

Dreeg couldn't understand my desperation to build my leg.

"Goodness me, just leave it, Luke. Why are you bothering? What's the point of twiddling a ball with your foot, anyway? How is it going to change the world?"

"Who gives a toss about that?"

"Wouldn't you like to?" asked Dreeg, surprised.

"Can't say it's my big ambition, no." I carried on trying to move the ball in smoother patterns.

"You can change the way people think, even what they see," said Dreeg. A worm slithered from his nose and slipped away. Why wasn't I surprised? His smile was slow honey.

"Why would I bother? What do I care what people think?"

Dreeg frowned. "You quite obviously don't have a clue what I'm talking about," he said crossly. "You probably think I'm talking about campaigns to save the whale or elephant or rain forest or greater spotted walrus or something. *Stop doing that!*" he shouted in exasperation. *"Listen to me!"*

I'd never heard him shout before. I stopped.

"Sorry," he said, shifting his greasy body slightly, with a sticky slapping sound like half-set glue. He tried to mold his face into interest. "Sorry. Tell me, Luke, what is it about running that's so special?"

I thought for a moment, looking deep into my head, and the computer screen reshaped before my eyes, full of possibilities. "It's the closest I'll ever come to flying. It's standing on the highest mountain, a million miles from anywhere, and shouting the whitest shout in the world. It's being light itself, the fastest thing in the universe, weightless. It's knowing you could touch a star, sucking speed from the Milky Way. It's sugared space dust bursting on the back of your tongue." And as I said it I felt it, melon sherbet singing through my veins.

"Run, Luke, run," urged Dreeg, daggers in his eyes. Eyes that were now the color of silver ice. Silver for temptation. Dreeg's appearance was now more human than ever before. No longer slumped, he stood tall and strong. Square-shouldered. Brilliant-eyed. And he gave me just what I wanted.

Without thinking, I stood up and walked, walked to the garden gate. I looked back at the house and then turned to the woods. I took off. Amber set off with me, barking in delight. We raced, Amber and I, and my legs were springs, steely-strong. Both legs. Over the spongy grass we sped, my arms pumping the air, my body weightless. Blown along. A dandelion seed. A laugh welled up inside me. A rich purple viola laugh of nothing but pleasure. Butterflies flew from my open mouth. Suddenly I couldn't feel my feet and when I looked down the ground was way way way below me.

I was flying.

Flying

I felt no fear as I flew. My silent scream was only the piercing laughter of a violin. At the top of a mountain I swooped briefly to trace the tips of my toes on the snow and then I was away again. From a million miles above a sapphire ocean I dived and caught with my tongue the froth on the spray of a wave. With my fingers I gathered one grain of sand from a desert and put it on my lip, where it burst into melon juice, and then I was away again, spearing the air, tumbling free, spiraling in whichever direction my thoughts flew. If I wanted to glide that way I thought of that way, and to soar up was nothing but an instant thought of upness. Yellow spangles showered from my fingertips and scattered around my head like fainting. Soon I spun with the planet— headfirst, or feetfirst, who knows?—seeing nothing but the thin gray lines of stretched objects, tasting the speed of the frosted wind in the gaps between my toes.

Backward in time as I flew, every sound that had ever been was squashed into the scream of a pin; every color melded into the taste of white; every atom of every thought blended into one perfectly spherical idea in my own head.

Whatever I wanted. I could have whatever I wanted. If I could fly, I could do anything. In the spice-white emptiness of my head as I flew through space at will, I realized the obvious: that if you can fly you can do anything. It's what everyone has dreamt of as a child. Adults don't dream of flying. They know better. But I could fly, so I could do anything.

Less than a gasp later I was landing with the lightness of a butterfly and, in a tumbled heap, I breathed in the warm apple grass as the space dust settled in my veins.

Dreeg was there with me, but what a different creature he was! In fact, although I said that it was Dreeg, I don't know how I knew. He was quite unrecognizable. Two arms and legs, just as you would hope for, strong, kind-looking and smelling of Big Mac and warm shortbread. And eyes, twinkling blue eyes with black pupils perfectly central. Silver-haired and clear-skinned, a hero armored by goodness. The way a god would look. If Dreeg could make me fly, then how more perfect could he be in my eyes? He was everything I wanted at that moment.

How could I ever have seen him differently? How could I have wanted him to disappear? How could I ever have doubted that he had everything I wanted?

"I ran," I said triumphantly. "And now do you see what's so brilliant about running?"

"You flew, actually," corrected Dreeg.

"It felt like flying," I said, already uncertain. "But how could it be flying?" Back on Earth, it didn't seem possible. I tried to catch the moment back again, to grasp its slippery realness. People don't really fly. The world just doesn't work like that.

"It was flying," he insisted with a smile. "I know you flew. That's what I've been talking about. That's what you can do now. That, and other things."

Amber arrived, panting after so much running. I held her, the realness of her. "What other things?"

"You've done a couple of them already. Remember in the hospital? You made Tom and the porter see your wheelchair differently. You changed the way they think, just by what you said, the way you described it. You changed the world for them."

"They were just being kind. It doesn't mean they really thought the wheelchair was a car."

"You think? But that's how they saw it. Briefly, but it was enough. To make it real enough. And then there was the insect. That wasn't just in their minds."

"What insect?"

"The one with the acid-green antennae?"

I thought back. There had been an insect on the floor of the hospital ward, I remembered.

"I don't know what you mean."

"Tom had a football in his hand when you came into the ward."

"Did he? I don't remember."

"Yes, he hid it behind his back when he saw the wheelchair. And did he have it when he left?"

I thought. He didn't.

Dreeg continued patiently. "On your screen. When you were in the wheelchair. I told you to do something."

"I don't know what I did, though. There were pictures and they seemed to move."

"Do you remember the insect?"

I struggled to think. "I saw it and then it jumped away. So? What did it do?"

"Come on! Think. Tom had a football. Then there was no football. There was no insect. Then there was an insect."

"The football turned into an insect. Oh, right!" I said sarcastically.

"Well, that would be to put it too literally. Let's just say that you wanted the ball not to be there, and you wanted it enough to be able to make it happen. You made it disappear. Or rather, you made it so that it hadn't been there."

This was too much. You might think it would be exciting to be told that you can change things by thinking about them, but I had realized that the problem was that if anything could happen, then everything could happen, and that, if you think about it, is weird. Nothing was reliable anymore. Sour rhubarb.

And yet . . . the power. To be able to fly.

"You can't really mean I can do absolutely anything at all?" Wanting and not wanting him to say no.

"There are conditions."

"Like?"

"First, you'll have to practice. Second, you may have to practice a lot. And third, you need me."

"Sounds great, I don't think."

"You flew, Luke." The sound of sherbet syrup rolling up my tongue.

"I can teach you to use this gift, Luke. This ability to see more than everyone else and to use language to control what is real. To do and have everything you want. To change anything, the world. We can change the world together, Luke, you and I. And remember—you can fly."

How could I refuse? Especially since I did not then know one important fact: that everything has a price. Who would pay the price for my flying?

The Girl at
the Crystal Pool

The next day, lagoon-blue Thursday, two more weird things happened. The second was that I wrote a poem. If only I hadn't, perhaps everything would have been all right.

You will know by now that I wasn't a poem-writing sort of person. Before my illness and the weirdness, I had been just an ordinary teenager. Sport, running, messing about with friends. But poems? Even Laura wouldn't do that, unless she had to, and Laura was supposed to be good at creative stuff.

Sometimes Roach, the English teacher, would read out bits of someone's poem or something that was meant to be "super, really super," but if you had any credibility you didn't write a poem of the sort that would be read out. You might try to make the lines rhyme for fun but that was it. To be honest, I didn't know what was so good about the ones that were read out.

Anyway, I wrote one. It was Dreeg's fault.

But first. The other weird happening.

Sticky heat that boiling blue Thursday. My head a melting toffee apple and the air humming heavy.

"Come with me," said Dreeg. "I'll show you something." I stopped kicking a ball against the wall and limped away from the house in the direction he wanted. I dripped and my pace slowed as I waded through the thick air. The deep sky bubbled above me and the caramel hills danced in the heat.

"Where am I going?" I grumbled, my leg more tired than I liked to admit.

"Look. Can't you see?"

"What? Where am I meant to be looking?"

"There. The crystal pool."

I screwed my eyes against the heat and looked along the dirt track, dusty. There were some trees not far away there was a pond I had often played dirty pond, nothing you would have pool.

"You haven't looked properly, Luke

"I've played there all my life. I kr just a pond with a tree hanging over ....king in the hot weather, too, mud more than water. Let's go back. I'm thirsty."

"You can drink from the pond, Luke. That's what I want to show you."

The pond looked just the same to me. Nasty.

"Imagine it beautiful. Want it like heaven. Long to drink from it. You are the thirstiest person who has ever lived. And you'll die if you don't drink." As he spoke, my eyes blurred as the computer screen came clear in front of me and through it the pond changed as I dragged and dropped the images darting inside my brain.

how luke uses his imaginatin

Ar[illegible]ol, bulrushes sway[illegible] they brushed me. F[illegible]nd of an oboe. Ghos[illegible]tte[illegible]ring over the cool lemonade po[illegible] drank a dragonfly, its color now wild blue, now spring green, as it shone petrol in the wet sunlight. Diamonds shimmered in the water, frozen sugar tasting, melting purple on my tongue as I drank.

I breathed out and soapy bubbles floated from my mouth, lifted on a sunbeam. And as I looked up from my pool, I saw her. On the far side of the crystal bowl, kneeling to drink like me, dressed in gossamer for the heat. Tangled in the golden curtain of her hair were musical notes, and the taste of ripest melon flooded my throat. From the ends of my fingers fluttered peppermint butterflies. She didn't look up. She didn't see me.

Suddenly she slipped. Now the water was black, ancient, grasping. Gone were the butterflies, the dragonfly, the lemonade diamond taste, the scent of melon. Now there were only chill air and the manic whisper of ghosts. Icy fingers closed my throat. I had to save her. As she slid toward the slimy blackness, scrabbling in the mud as her feet disappeared below the water, I started to run to her, calling out that I was coming. My leg was strong and clear. Easy. Steel-spring strong.

I pushed through the brambles around the edge of the pond, not feeling their thorns. She was sliding down, nothing to cling on to, fingers digging into the mud, gasping. Almost up to her thighs in the black, quick-silt water. I forced the speed of a cheetah into my legs. Ran. Faster and faster. Feet flying above the ground. I knew I would reach her in time.

But suddenly, without warning, something changed inside me. Heaviness seeped through my muscles. In a moment I was slowed to a crawl. My feet were being sucked into the mud, glue setting around them. Desperately I grabbed a branch to pull myself out. But my strength was going and there was nothing I could do as I fell facedown on the riverbank.

My vision had slipped and the screen was moving back. I knew now that I had no chance of reaching her. I heard her scream.

And on the Sixth Day . . .

I looked up. She had grabbed a branch and stopped her slide, without me. With strong arms she pulled herself, dripping, up the bank and, without a glance in my direction, began to run. Fast as a deer she disappeared into the sunlight.

The pond was back to normal, small, stinking and not fit for drinking. I wiped my lips where they were still wet. A diamond glistened on the back of my hand.

I looked at Dreeg. "What was that?"

"That was what you did. With my help, of course. I opened your mind to some ideas, but you did it. Turned the water into lemonade. Made the girl. Even made her slip. Only, then you lost control, didn't you?" He grinned at me, knowingly. "You wanted to save her, didn't you? So why didn't you? Why did you wait for her to save herself? You could have played the hero."

"I don't know what you're talking about. It was just what happened, that's all. She just caught the branch and saved herself. I couldn't get there in time."

"Not trying hard enough!" laughed Dreeg, teasing. "If it hadn't been for me she'd have fallen in. Some hero you are, even when you write the story yourself!"

He looked at my question mark. "Sit down," he said. In the ginger heat I sat and he began to talk.

"Things are not the same for you as they were before. Something has happened in your brain and you experience things differently. And you've already discovered that it's not just about how you see things. You've also seen the beginnings of how you can use this gift. But you can do much, much more than you have done so far. You can do anything you want, have anything, things no one else in the world can do. Just as you thought that moment when you flew— it's true. You can have it all. What does that feel like?" His fanatic eyes glowed and the warmth of them cocooned me.

What did it feel like? Losing control. Fainting. Standing on the top of the world and being outside it. Yet owning it.

"Scary." Like a snake growing in the darkness.

"Oh, so, you don't want it?" His scathing voice cut into me. "Well, if you don't want it, Luke, just say the word and you can make it go away. You can have normal back if that's what you really want." His sarcasm hurt me, put my hackles up, made me want to hit back.

"I can? How?"

"Just say so. Just tell me."

"Just like that? Now if I want to?" Did I really want to?

"You have to mean it, though. And you have to prove to me that you really mean it, that you really want things to be as they were before. That you don't want this fantastic . . .

power." He rolled the word *power* stickily around his mouth like softened chocolate.

"What do you mean, prove?"

"Fly once more, one last time, and then tell me that you don't want it anymore. That you want it all back to normal. That you want to be stagnant-ditchwater ordinary, the same as everyone else. That you want to leave your useless leg to nature. That you never want to fly again. Then I'll go. Willingly leave you to your own pathetic ordinary devices."

I thought about it. Tossed the choices in my head. Back to normal? Or everything else?

I used to think that people in fairy stories were stupid. You know, when they are given three wishes, why don't they think of using the last one to wish for endless wishes? Everything you want, on a plate, forever. Well, now I know power doesn't work like that. It does something to the balance of the world. Power should be spread about evenly but if it's all lumped up in one place, or with one person, the earth wobbles out of control. But I didn't know that then.

Dreeg, a lemony halo round him, continued, goading, pushing and pulling me at the same time. "Go on, liver breath. Little boy with the guts of frog spawn. Do it now. Come on, fly with me and tell me that you don't want this power."

Still I could not choose between the two-faced images in my head. On the screen crawled cakes and marshmallow snakes. Poisonous scaly bats with angels' wings and strawberry tarts with slug-juice trails. How could I choose? Then there was the feeling of flying, touching the stars and skimming the ocean, Tom and the racing car–wheelchair, the sunbeams dancing on lemonade water, power. Power. The weird wonderful idea of being able to do anything. And the girl, fascinating, never close enough. Something in the way her hair fell and her skin sang and in the scent of her strength as she ran.

"I want it. I want you to stay."

The metal-masked man hissed in the forest and licked his lips. I saw the smell of roasting. I heard a dead tulip petal fluttering onto a grave.

Dreeg puffed with pleasure and a wasp flew from his mouth, buzzing around my face before flying away. His face smiled on one side and stayed motionless on the other. I didn't know this at the time, but it's what people do when they are hiding something.

Dreeg continued, shivering with the excitement of having my agreement at last.

"OK, so let's get down to some practice. You've got to learn to control what happens in your head or it will control you. That's mainly what's been happening so far. The computer screen is your box of tools. Let your eyes drift. Bring the screen clearly in front of you. Good, good. That's it. Now, what do you want?"

"The girl." I could hear him snigger. I looked at him. He was fattening in front of me, his eyes yellowing and skin drying. Was there some unseen part deep inside me that didn't like what he was doing? Perhaps I should have listened to it.

"So sorry," he said. "OK, the girl. Think about her. Be creative, forget ordinary stuff like blue eyes or smooth skin. Twist the senses, stretch the meaning, find a combination never used before, challenge me to understand, spark my imagination, invade me."

In a trance, as my eyes swam over, I spoke. "Her skin is cinnamon in the sun, cake-warm, her hair long as honey. She flows like cream, blows candy-floss bubbles in the air. Runs like tomorrow, whispers one day, promises never. Her distant touch is soft as smoke, deep as a breath. I dream her taste and feel the sounds of strawberries on my fingers. Silent in her head, she melts toward me and I only fear she is not there."

And she did. Come toward me. I didn't know what to say, being only an ordinary boy who doesn't know what to say to girls. But as she came closer I could see she hadn't seen me, sitting as I was in the long grass. On an impulse, I stood up and then she did see me. She smiled distantly, turned slightly and carried on walking on a path that would take her past me a short way away. When she was close enough, I tried to say "Hello" but it came out as a mouse's squeak so I said it again, louder.

Her face remained still, as though she had not heard. But she was close enough that she must have heard, though I could see no blush, no reflex turning away, none of the signs of a girl who is pretending not to hear. The tips of my fingers fizzed with her closeness. A few steps and I could have touched her warm skin.

There was something about her limpid stillness, something about the depth of her silence as she passed me. Suddenly, I knew what it was, knew it from inside me.

Power Failure

The girl I had conjured up was deaf.

I would have followed her but when I tried to walk, my head went limp and a nauseous ache brought me to my knees. The fear of ending up in hospital again made me lie in the grass until the nausea passed.

Who was the girl with the cinnamon skin? Was she real? She had to be. I had to find her again.

That afternoon I wrote the poem. About the girl. Because Dreeg told me to. I wrote it pretty much as I had spoken it, ignoring the rules I thought you had to follow for writing poems. Just flowed it out, like bleeding. Yes, it felt silly but Dreeg said I didn't have to show it to anyone. That it could be just for me. That it was just a practice run at creating things. Changing the world, as he kept putting it annoyingly.

I could do it in my head, he said, but then it wouldn't be so real, might just be a bubble to burst in my thoughts. So I wrote it out as a poem, for myself, just to make the girl more real.

But there was a problem. The problem was that Laura found the poem. I had been writing it in the garden and I had only gone into the house because Mum shouted that Grandpa was on the phone for me.

"Don't go," said Dreeg, impatient for me to finish my creation. "Tell him you'll phone him back."

But I hobbled into the house.

Grandpa is kind and twinkling, bad in the best sense. A wicked way with words and quite likely to slip five pounds into my hand for the smallest reason. He smells of sweet tobacco and jazz.

"How's it going, then?" he asked.

"Oh, you know, boring."

"What about the old leg? You running yet?" Grandpa would always get straight to the point, no faffing around and pretending not to know about something.

"Nah, prefer flying. I can fly now, you know?"

"Really? Now, that's something! How about you come and stay with me for a while sometime and show me your flying? Thought you might like to miss the last week of term. Your mother doesn't mind. In the circumstances, she said."

And I wouldn't be around when sports day came and went, of course. Which was probably the point.

"You'll miss your school sports day, of course, but I thought you'd prefer not to be there. You won't be running, I hear. Not this year. No time to get that leg strong enough. But don't you worry—I'll soon get you fit for next year."

Somehow when Grandpa said it like that, so matter-of-fact, it was easy to believe. And one thing he was right about: I didn't want to be at sports day if I couldn't run. And win.

Then I remembered: I could do anything I wanted! I could fly, I could run faster than imagination, just by conjuring it up like a magician. I could magic myself better and then everyone would be amazed when they saw me, limping Luke, hobble to the starting line and flash toward the finish.

But for now, what should I say to Grandpa? No, actually, Grandpa, I *am* going to sports day because just by the power of the words in my head I can run faster than the fastest runner in the universe. And in fact I'll be fit for the interschools competition, too, and I'll win a gold medal. Yes, part of my brain has been damaged but another part has grown and I can actually create things, like a god. Oh, and by the way, I have this person in my head who helps me and sometimes he's the ugliest slime you can imagine and at others he's the coolest, most mesmerizing, strongest person you could dream of being.

No, I had to work out a realistic way of putting Grandpa off.

"That'd be brilliant, Grandpa," I said. "I don't know what the teachers will say, though. What about the first week of the holidays?"

"No can do, I'm afraid. I'm going away the week after that. Portugal. Golfing." White, crimson, chrome, gold, yellow, mint, puce, pink, the letters of *Portugal* flooded my head. "Since when did you worry what the teachers might say, Luke?"

"I must still be ill," I joked.

"So you'll come, then?"

I had to say yes. Adults always want logical reasons. He chattered on about the things we would do, while I reassured myself inside that what I would do would be to get fit unbelievably soon, so that Mum would be able to tell Grandpa that I was running on sports day after all. Then Grandpa could come and watch me win and I could go back with him afterward for a couple of days. And everyone would be happy. Just like before.

I could almost believe that it might work.

But it didn't happen like that because at that moment I heard a neigh of laughter from the garden. Laura!

I knew what had happened. Dreeg's face dissolved into mash. A cloud of bluebottles swarmed around him, laying their eggs on the dissolving quicksand of his skin. I dropped the phone and ran.

Before I could reach the front door, Laura had come into the house waving a piece of paper above her head. My poem. She came toward me cackling, the angry wasps swarming round her face.

"Cinnamon skin, warm as cake! Who is this vision, Luke? This girl who, what was it, 'flows like cream'? Wooooooo, boyfriend. Who's got the hots then, Lukey baby?"

"Shut up, you cow!" I tried to grab the paper as she ran past me into the kitchen but how could I? My leg put me at a disadvantage and she was taller than me. "It's nothing! Just some schoolwork."

"Oh, you aren't trying to tell me you *wrote* it? Come on, Luke, who do you take me for? Roach will never believe you, you know. 'I dream her taste and feel the sounds of strawberries on my fingers.' Oh, puh-leeze! It's a love poem. Little boys don't write poems like that. Don't have feelings like that."

She darted round the table, always out of reach of my fury. Over and over again she recited my poem, in a gooey fake peach voice. Breathless, I stopped at the end of the table and with massive effort gathered together the bits of my brain.

"Who's the lucky lucky girl, Lukey baby?" she asked.

I spoke steel. "She's no one. It's a made-up piece of rubbish." And suddenly I couldn't see the deaf girl in my mind anymore. Could only remember her mistily. She was fading into breath.

"Yes, well, if you wrote it, it is rubbish. And if she likes you, she is no one."

Dreeg was a rotten corpse, with cockroach eyes. I hated him for what he had done.

I had never wanted to hurt Laura as much as I did then. I could have done the worst thing in the world and not imagined regretting it later. Yet, in the very next micromoment, I realized that this was a horrifying thought. How had I become like this?

Lizard green, the memory leapt at me again. Boys laughing, as I drowned in the smell of disinfectant, urine and vomit. Something in the boys' toilets. That's where it was. Something angry in the boys' toilets. Fear, too. But I still couldn't catch what it was. It slid slipperily away. I couldn't see Dreeg. Where was he when I needed him? I would have to deal with it myself.

I took a deep breath, bringing up the computer screen in

front of me. "Read it again, Laura, read it and listen to the words. You're supposed to be so good at language—but perhaps this is over your head. Go on, read it out and tell me what you see."

As she read, I focused desperately on the computer screen, sorting, concentrating. If I couldn't make something happen now, when I really wanted to, then what was the point of any of it? I tried to bring the girl back, to make her real as Laura read my words.

It didn't work on her. As she read, she laughed, twisting my thoughts into a joke, wiggling her hips and pouting her slug-lips so that all the meaning just vanished on her spit. Nothing happened at all. Except that my anger burst.

I picked up a vase and threw the stale green water over her. She gasped as it plastered her head and trickled stinking through her mascara. Spitting, she ran from the kitchen, snarling, "You snotty little git. You'll bloody regret that. I'll get you for that."

And the man with the metal mask watched her from the darkness, grinning as he whispered, "I'll get you, dirty little slut. When I want to, I'll get you."

Who was this man in the darkness? In my blind fury I paused only briefly to wonder. Where had he come from and what was he doing? He seemed to have come from a place deeper and darker in my head than I had ever known was there. When you look into a cave, at first you see very little. But as you get used to the darkness, you see more and more. If you dare stay long enough, eventually you see everything.

Ice Cream

"**It didn't work!**" I yelled at Dreeg, now a jellyfish with a trillion yellow eyes. "Why didn't it work, you slimeball?" I limped up to my room and slammed the door but he was there first, always with me, everywhere.

"I don't know," he said. I was too angry to work out whether I believed him or to look at his face.

"Oh, and I thought you knew everything! I thought you said I could do anything! You said I would make the girl more real if I wrote the words. So why didn't Laura see her, then? What the hell's the point if only I can see her?"

"It's not my fault, you know," replied Dreeg. "I don't know everything. I'm in *your* head, remember. Besides, I did say you'd have to practice."

"Well, it bloody stinks. You bloody stink. Look at you squatting there like a dog turd. What do you mean you don't know everything, anyway? I thought you were the great god who knows it all. I did exactly what you said and now look what's happened. God knows what she'll do now."

"You threw the water on her, Luke. I didn't do that. And I did tell you not to go and answer the phone. She wouldn't have found the poem if you had done as I said," Dreeg snapped self-righteously, scraping the scurf from under a fingernail.

"You told me to write the damn poem. You said it would make the girl real."

"She is real. Just that Laura didn't see her. Didn't want to see her, was too caught up in teasing you. Maybe you should have written it differently for her."

"I didn't write it for Laura, you stupid . . . whatever grossness you are."

"So? Who did you write it for?"

"Me. I wrote it for me."

"And the girl was real . . . to you?"

"Yes . . . no . . . I don't know. You tell me."

"Well. She seemed pretty real to me. I could smell her, even. Cinnamon, you said."

"Yes, but you're in my head so what does that mean?"

"Maybe you'll just have to find out what it means."

"Maybe I just won't bother. Maybe I'll just tell you to go."

"Give up now, you mean? After just one setback? Are you saying that this is it, then, that you want to fly one more time, one more magic moment, and then it all goes? Back to normal?"

I wanted to say yes, wanted to say that I had had enough and wanted none of this weirdness anymore. But I stayed silent, fizzing. Dreeg continued, "Besides, if you give up now, you'll still have the problem of Laura. She will still be furious with you in any case. And you'll have no weapons to use, no power. Think of all the things you want to do. To run, to win, to meet the girl again. To harm, punish Laura. You won't be able to do those things on your own."

"I never said anything about harming Laura. Where did you get that?"

"You do, though, don't you? You hate her—admit it. You'd love something nasty to happen to her. Death by some gruesome method. Eaten by spiders, perhaps. Roasted on a spit."

"Don't be stupid. Of course I wouldn't. So she bugs me till my teeth grind but that's a long way from wanting her to die." Metal man breathing deeply in the dark, waiting with shrinking patience. Smoke, flames, someone dying.

"Why, Luke? Why do you hate her so much? Where does it come from?"

"There's no why. It's just a brother-sister thing. It's no big deal. Look at her, how she dresses, how she walks. How she acts like a slag." I was barricading myself in. I would not discuss it with him. How could I, when I didn't understand myself?

Pine. Ammonia. Graffiti-green walls.

"So? It's what they do at that age. You're hiding something. What are you hiding in there? What's she done?" His eyes, night-black now, drilled into me like screwdrivers. The vinegar squeak of polystyrene.

"I'm not hiding anything."

"What's she done, Luke?" Dreeg goaded. His words nipped at my eyelids, like ants.

"Nothing."

"Can't be nothing. She must have done something. Unless you're plain mad or bad, of course. If she's done nothing, then she should be the one who hates you for how you are to her. I can see a shadow in your head. That's where your memory is. She did something and you know it."

Dreeg's nicotine fingers scraped away at the soil in my head and planted a tiny seed. He dribbled to water it.

"I don't know anything. Stop going on at me. You don't know what you're talking about."

"If you say so." Dreeg suddenly seemed to lose interest. He had a knack of changing the subject, changing the whole tone of his face in an instant but leaving the thoughts hanging in space. "Anyway, back to the matter in hand. We were talking about what you wouldn't be able to do if I wasn't in your life. So, let's leave aside what you do or don't want to do to Laura—and why. For now. What about the other stuff you want? You can't have any of it if you fly with me and turn it all down."

"At this rate, it doesn't look as though I'm going to have any of it, anyway, even with your so-called help. I mean, let's look at the facts. Most of the time my leg's still rubbish, there's no way I'm going to be fit by sports day and certainly not for the interschools comp, there are weird pictures in my head which I can't control at all, I can't control what Laura thinks or does, I can't make Seraphina stay long enough to speak to me—"

"Seraphina?"

"The girl by the pool."

"You know her name now? That makes her quite real, I'd say."

I don't know how I knew her name. It was just something

that was in my head as soon as I needed it and yet it felt as though it had always been there.

"In my head. Not out there."

"In your head is where things start. That's where I—" He stopped himself suddenly. "Where I know you can start to change the world."

"Oh, changing the world! That's all you're interested in!"

"Quite important, I'd say," replied Dreeg.

"But *so* not interesting, that's what you don't understand, you who think you know everything. So not interesting, you wouldn't believe it."

"Well, what interests you? What exactly do you want out of your life? Apart from harming Laura, sorry, not harming Laura." Dreeg looked at me patronizingly.

"I want an ice cream. I want an enormous ice cream spangled with orange crispy bits. Bright orange like a fireball, with a chocolate umbrella piercing it. I want fudge sauce dripping from it onto a mint-wafer bowl. I want a violet fountain of sherbet to spurt out when I bite into it."

And there it was in front of me, just as I had described it. At that moment the doorbell rang and a moment later Mum let Tom into my bedroom.

"Don't eat ice cream in your room," said Mum. "That's a weird concoction, anyway. What do you call that? Vesuvius? You'd better make one for Tom," she added as she went out.

"Cool!" said Tom.

What was I going to do now? "It's OK, you have it," I said. "I'm not really hungry anymore."

"Coward," sneered Dreeg.

"Cool!" said Tom, his eyes widening. His innocence, his

total acceptance of this miracle, terrified me. It made me feel alone and vulnerable. If only I could tell him a part of what was happening to me. But then he would have seen my difference. I needed him to stay the same, something for me to attach myself to in all this craziness.

"Coward!" whispered Dreeg again, his spittle landing in my ear. "Why not make another one? Don't you dare?"

"We'd better go downstairs," I said to Tom.

We went down, me using the banister to disguise my limp, and Dreeg chanting, "Chicken legs! Soft as eggs! Daddy's little bunny-pegs!" Insects crawling.

We went into the kitchen. Tom sat down at the table and started his ice cream. I wondered what it would taste like—after all, it wasn't really supposed to be there. Zinging orange, I sincerely hoped.

"Wow! Zinging orange!" he breathed in amazement.

"I think I'll have one after all," I said, and went with jittery heart to the freezer, where I took out a tub of vanilla ice cream. I closed my eyes and muttered a sort of abracadabra-type thing. Opened my eyes. Vanilla. Plain. Bit melted round the edges.

"I think we've run out of the orange flavor," I said. "Never mind, vanilla's fine."

"Yellow-belly! Lily-liver!" jeered Dreeg.

Sharing Cells

I kept my eyes open and brought the screen into focus. Breathed, wanted, created—and there was my enormous ice cream spangled with orange crispy bits. Bright orange like a fireball, with a chocolate umbrella piercing it, fudge sauce dripping from it onto a mint-wafer bowl. A violet fountain of sherbet ready to spurt out when I bit into it. Easy as anything when you know how.

Tom was too engrossed in his ice cream to notice how quickly my Vesuvius had appeared.

"When are you coming back to school?" he wanted to know.

"Monday." Bleeding-nose Monday.

"How's your leg?" Tom said, concentrating on his ice cream, a tiny frown at the corner of his eyes.

"Getting better. Getting better every day. I might make sports day." I didn't mention that I was still aiming for the interschools competition, too. That might seem a bit far-fetched. After all, it was only a little more than two weeks away.

Tom was desperate to believe me and his face lit up. "Cool! That's great! I thought . . . well, I thought you couldn't."

"My physio says it's possible. If I really work hard and build up my strength. Probably won't win, but at least I'll run." No one had said any such thing. No one had said anything about it at all. No one really bothered about whether I would run in any competition. Compared with surviving meningitis, it wasn't important to them. The fact that I existed was enough for them. But I wanted more and I had realized that I was prepared to steal it if necessary. Do anything.

"Come to athletics tomorrow. Not to race. Just to do some fitness training."

Scary idea. Everyone looking at me. The boy who'd had meningitis. The boy who can't run properly anymore. But I would have to do it sometime.

"I'll ask Mum. I might not be allowed."

We spent some easy time, messing around with our ice creams, laughing about school stuff, changing the ring tones on our mobile phones. I felt lighter than I had for days. Tom was treating me like normal, so I could almost believe that I was.

Dreeg just watched from a distance. With his eyes a new shade of hollow green, he stared at Tom, as if weighing him up, measuring him. That was when I realized that Dreeg did not like my best friend.

Laura disappeared to school next morning before I saw her. I was enjoying my last weekday lie-in. I hadn't seen her since she'd stormed out dripping the day before. She had spent the evening closed in her room, apparently working, though why when her exams were finished I hadn't the faintest idea. She always was a swot, though. Apple of every teacher's eye, worm of mine. It beats me how no one else can ever see what she is really like.

It tormented me that she shared my cells. That if I ever had to have a bone marrow transplant to save my life, she would probably be the closest match in the whole universe. That if a scientist examined even one tiny cell of my body and one tiny cell of hers, he would discover that we were more the same than any other two of the six billion people on the planet.

We weren't always like this. I could remember playing together like any brother and sister when we were younger. I could remember her helping me learn to read. I even used to enjoy being with her. She was tough, not afraid to learn tricks on a bike or skateboard. She used to think I was worth talking to, that I meant something. When we fought, it was like boys fighting, fists and rolling on the ground. She didn't run away crying like some girls. Then that changed, but only slowly, in normal ways, and before long we sniped with words instead of fists when we argued. Mum and Dad would call us frightful teenagers, and that was really all it was. Now it was very different and I didn't know why.

I said before that it had changed when I woke up in hospital, but that's not entirely true. Certainly, the slugs and wasps and the viperous acid taste when I looked at her— they all started then. But before that, weeks or months before that, it seemed to me that Laura had been changing then, though slowly. The slaggy, tarty look, the makeup, the skirt riding up her legs, the creep boyfriend. Something dirty in his eyes.

As soon as I thought of him, saliva rushed to my mouth as the smell of disinfectant came again. A pain in my head just where the shadow was. The memory was there, stronger now. In it I was kneeling on a concrete floor with a spear in my head, vomiting, and around me the stink of laughing voices. Paul. The sound of rushing water and my head hitting the cold floor with a dead black thud.

When the flashback was over, I felt sick. I lay back on my pillows and closed my eyes.

Was this the memory Dreeg was talking about? If so, how did it involve Laura? I couldn't see her there. It was the boys' toilets, after all. What about the voices? Perhaps one of them was hers? Part of me wanted to catch this memory properly but another part of me wanted to bury it forever. Dreeg had planted a seed in my head and the roots were beginning to swell and tangle their jellyfish strands. It was true: I did hate Laura. I had thought it was just normal stuff but now I knew there was something extra. Something to do with this memory that kept almost coming back.

Somewhere else in my head, not far away, the man with the metal mask laughed silently in the darkness. He held a bunch of black tulips in his white-gloved hand and the ribbon that tied them was a snake. In the distance, I heard the faintest screams of a forest fire.

Working the Magic

My leg was getting stronger. It was still a bit fuzzy round the edges but if I concentrated very hard, I could almost make even that disappear for short periods. Organizing the pictures on the screen, focusing on the thought of a machine and its smooth clockwork mechanism, its balance, I could walk without a limp. On the treadmill, the physiotherapist switched the speed up gradually till I had to do a lolloping jog. At first this was hard, but if I pressed liquid gold into my leg muscles, I could do it. I wasn't going to win a race like that but I was running. Getting better every day. Almost believable. Whereas flying would most certainly not be.

"Great stuff, Luke! I never thought you'd get this far so fast," said the physio. "What has your mum been feeding you?"

"Volcanoes," I said. "Can I go to athletics this evening?"

"Well, I'm not sure that's a good idea." He saw my face sink. "You've been ill. You can't push it too fast."

"I've been pushing it and I feel fine. You said yourself

how well I was doing. I can run on sports day. There's still more than three weeks and look what I've done in a week." I didn't mention the interschools competition.

"You're building up your muscles. But it wasn't your muscles that were damaged. It takes longer for your brain to adapt."

"You don't know anything about my brain."

"Not much to know, is there?" he joked.

"Let me go to athletics training. I promise I won't do too much. I want to see everyone."

He let me go. He had a word with Mum in private so I don't know what he said but I expect it was something like "It's just to keep his spirits up. Tell the coach not to push him too hard, but some gentle fitness training will be fine. He'll feel his life's getting back to normal."

Normal. What did he know?

I sent Tom a text message. "c u @ athletix!" and a smiley face.

He sent one back. "kool!!" and two smiley faces.

I began to forget about the poem. I shouldn't have.

Athletics training that evening. Better than the ice cream, almost better than the flying.

I was careful not to fly instead of running. It would have caused complications. Besides, my distance is 800 meters and for that, flying is not necessary.

"Good to see you, Luke. You feeling better now?" Mr. Breslin was casually welcoming. Tom grinned when he saw me and ran over to hit me on the back.

It felt good to join in the warm-up with everyone else,

though I admit that I felt weaker than I'd expected. Dreeg sat quietly on the sidelines of my mind, looking ill at ease as I surrounded myself in all this physical activity. I smiled to myself. This was my world. This was where I fitted, not in the world of poetry writing and weird words.

I focused my screen, moved the cursor onto Dreeg and slowly dragged him toward the wastebin. He was heavy. More to the point, he started to dissolve and melt, so that it was impossible to drag him. He kept slipping like an octopus out of my grasp. I left him lying in a pool of himself and colored him in green so that he blended with the grass and I could entirely ignore him.

I persuaded Mr. Breslin to let me run an 800, not as a race, I said. Just for fun. I wouldn't push myself, I promised. He looked doubtful, but no teacher can resist a boy actually asking to work hard, so of course he said I could.

We started, everyone trying to achieve that delicate balance between setting off too fast and needing to stay within reach of the front. My leg was worse than I'd expected, weaker than earlier in the day, and my head was beginning to ache again. Very soon I was starting to fall behind, dragged back by this leaden limb, which seemed to have lost its strength. I couldn't find the computer screen at all and I couldn't see Dreeg. Surely I could do better than this? But no matter how I tried, the other boys were pulling ahead and I was running in sand.

Dreeg waved a green tentacle at me from his hole, still in the octopus shape I had made for him. "Is that all you can do, Luke?"

"Do something useful," I gasped. "Don't just squat there."

"Need me now, do you? I said you would. You still need me, you see."

"Yes, yes, yes, all right, so I need you. I can't help it if there's something wrong with my leg."

Dreeg re-formed into an almost human shape and sat there, grinning smugly. "On you go, then, Luke, go for it. Think it, feel it, live it."

Dissolved my eyes, looked into my head, found the computer screen. Focused on being as light as air. Smelt cotton wool and rocket fuel as I ran. Power seeped back.

Quickly I passed three runners, then another. Heard the rasping breath of the next as I swooped past him. There were three more boys in front of me. A million tiny springs lifted my feet. My lungs expanded, sucking in oxygen and sending it whooshing round my body, quick like silver, lemonade-tasting. Chasing a sherbet rainbow, I passed the others, hearing only the sound of an eagle diving. I couldn't hear Mum telling me to go easy, didn't know Mr. Breslin was shouting "Come on, Luke!" As I crossed the line, a bubble burst blue in my head and I collapsed, almost fainting for less than a second. When I opened my eyes, Dreeg was standing there, looking faintly absurd with shining white wings and a golden syrup glow.

"Marvelous, marvelous, Luke!" Mr. Breslin was shouting as he examined his stopwatch. "Absolutely marvelous!"

"What were you thinking of?" Mum was saying, with jelly in her voice as she helped me up. "I told you to take it easy. You'll be ill again." The one thing that worried her.

"I'm fine. I'm totally fine." And I was. Better than fine. Perfect. Amazing. Like flying.

Well, I was picked for the interschools team, though Mr. Breslin had to promise Mum that if she said I wasn't well enough by then, I wouldn't run. I would be well enough, though. I could fly, after all. I could do anything, anything at all. As long as I had Dreeg to help me.

Cheat! said an ugly voice in my head. Acid pepper taste.

As we drove home, with Dreeg stroking his white hair in the softening sun, I struggled again with the niggling doubt: that it was cheating to win like this. I'm no goody-goody but I'm not a cheat. Or at least, I never used to be. But then I'd never before had temptation like this, the opportunity to use an extraordinary power.

No, it was *me,* without outside help, I replied to this doubt as I tried to push it away. My legs, *my* strength, *my* creative power.

But could you do it without Dreeg? nagged the doubt. Could you do it without his help?

I had to admit that I couldn't. With help, I was a cheat. Without help, I was nothing but a boy with a weak leg. A boy who wanted to win more than anything else. What did a boy like that do when faced with the choice of cheating or losing? What would anyone do? Although by now I was beginning to see the problem with power, I hadn't properly learnt what it meant. Like being told something and kind of half-believing it, but not having discovered the truth of it. People need proof before they can really believe in danger. Unfortunately, by then it's too late.

Back to School

On **Monday morning** I went back to school. It sounds so easy when I say it like that. Just the sort of thing you usually do on a day of that color.

As I got dressed, I sent Tom a text message. "skool 2day. c u on bus." And five minutes later came the reply, two smiley faces.

Laura and I had no choice but to take the same bus to school. There was only one that went through our village. There had been a time when she sat with me, but that was the past. Since she had changed, and my feelings toward her had changed, we ignored each other completely at the bus stop and I always pushed on first and sat at the front. Today Tom, running out of his house at the last minute, joined me as always and, as always, we wrestled for the window seat. I lost, but it didn't matter. Laura sat at the back and took out her makeup mirror while she waited for her boyfriend to get on the bus a few stops later.

Here he was. Horribly tall. Gel in his licked-back hair.

The sports bag draped over his shoulder hit me as he slouched past. "So sorry," he said, mocking. He walked on down the bus to Laura. I didn't look round but I could hear the giggling, saw the driver look in his mirror, tut and do nothing.

The sick green flashback again. Stronger now. Words, clashing words. A bursting anger in my head, the heat of it agony. Somewhere me hitting something, someone. Then a roar, being picked up, my head held underwater and laughter as the toilet was flushed over my face. And me vomiting, the cold thud of the floor and blackness again. Followed by dizzy ambulance noises.

It was coming back. But what was it about? What was the anger for? And what did it have to do with Laura? I still couldn't quite grasp the whole memory, put it into words.

At school that day I was "the boy who nearly died from meningitis." You could see the curiosity in people's faces. Not one teacher shouted at me all day.

English. Roach, a man who has never washed his hair and keeps yellow creatures in his fingernails, sat on the edge of his desk as he waited for us to settle. Dreeg jumped up and down in anticipation. Today his eyes were burnt amber, bright with excitement. I was happy for him to be there—he could see how I was in the real world of school. My world.

We are, as a class, neither especially well-behaved nor especially bad, but Roach is a teacher we choose not to annoy. He is not particularly strict, but he has a well-known tendency to spit when he is excited, which can happen either when he has read something that he considers to be powerful writing or when he is angry. And he has ferret breath. He owns one jacket, which is dry-cleaned during the holidays. We know this because each first day of term, it is stiff and strong, ready for anything, but as the term goes on it sags with him, tiring of the gray weight of teaching us.

"Fear!" he bellowed today as soon as we were quiet, forming his hands into claws and pretending to frighten us. We looked at each other as he continued. "Fear! What is fear to you? What frightens you? You, Mark? Tell me what frightens you," and he pointed at Mark.

"The dark," replied Mark, quite reasonably, but we all laughed, for no good reason.

"Yes, the dark. Most people are frightened of the dark," agreed Roach, "even if they don't admit it. Cobwebs, graveyards, skeletons, ghosts. What about the rest of you?"

Silence and some shuffling.

"Come on, I want all the frightening things you can think of."

Someone shouted out, "Earthquakes!" Then everyone joined in. The ideas came faster. Fire, drowning, water, torture, aliens, pain, monsters with green eyes, Mr. Roach . . . some laughter at this.

And into the laughter I shouted what I could see in my head through the screen, "Watching a seesaw in an empty playground. It is moving slowly up and down. Squeaking. The seesaw stops and a fistful of leaves lifts and blows directly toward you. Slowly."

There was silence and they looked at me. Charlotte had turned white and no one blinked. A chill passed by like a ghost and I could hear a slow squeak coming from somewhere in the room.

Traitor

Roach looked at me in surprise and rubbed his hands. "Excellent, Luke. A truly frightening idea. You see, everyone, it doesn't have to be the monsters and ghouls with green eyes which frighten us most. Sometimes the sense that there might be something there, something out there waiting to get us, can be the most chilling of all."

Roach continued to drone on with some examples of frightening stories from literature.

A piece of screwed-up paper landed on my desk. I unfolded it on my lap.

"Suck up." I didn't know who had thrown it.

Dreeg squelched as he shifted. "Ignore it, Luke. It's not worth it." He was on my side.

Homework was to write a frightening story. We were allowed to start in class, which is what teachers usually do when they haven't prepared enough for the lesson. I couldn't concentrate, couldn't put my thoughts together.

My head ached and I wished I was at home. I stared out of the window and chewed my pen. I could see the woods from where I sat. Sometimes I walked home through the woods instead of getting the bus.

"Luke Patterson! You won't get anywhere at all by looking out of the window!" said Roach, in a voice that normally would have been stinging but today was a soft cello. The dying brown smell of damp moss floated across my tongue.

"Just looking for inspiration, Mr. Roach," I replied.

"Yes, well, hurry up and find some," he said.

"Silly man," muttered Dreeg. "Doesn't he realize that inspiration is worth waiting for? Doesn't he understand creative genius? How dare he speak to my boy with so little respect?"

I smiled. "He's just a teacher, Dreeg! It's only homework!"

"Ah, but it could be so much more," sighed Dreeg. "If you wanted it to be. It could be everything."

The day continued. A few girls gave me funny looks after English, but generally speaking I started to feel more normal. Disguising the limp all the time was impossible and the best I could do was to walk slowly and concentrate hard on the pictures of strength inside my head. But it's hard to concentrate on controlling what is in your head at the same time as having a normal conversation in the normal world. If I wanted to do stuff with the screen, creative stuff, I had to focus completely on that and I couldn't do anything else at the same time.

My friends, of course, ignored my limp and waited for me when I walked slowly. But there were others who stared at me. Laura was no better. She slouched against a wall with boyfriend Paul. As I limped past, Paul said, quite loudly, "Cripple!" and I'm sure Laura laughed.

As I moved further away I distinctly heard him say, "And you say that's brain damage? Weird."

By now I knew that the flashback was coming. I smelt it, felt the nausea as it rushed through my tired brain. But maddeningly, I still couldn't get the words. Or what had happened before.

Tom was looking at me. "You all right?"

I shook the image away. "Yes, fine. That creep, that's all. Laura's boyfriend. I want to get him. I hate him. Both of them." A sickening waft of roasting. Dreeg rubbing his hands. Dreeg understood. I could see it in his eyes, now as clear as diamonds, and the softness of his face and the way he turned his wise head on one side as he stood a little behind my thoughts, supporting.

"Your sister's all right," said Tom. "Great legs." He was looking at Laura. At her long legs under the too-short skirt.

Dreeg sucked in his breath. I felt sick. "She's a tart. Get your filthy eyes off her and never speak like that again." Before my eyes could betray me, I limped away from Tom toward the classroom. He came after me, hurt and surprise in his voice.

"Come off it, Luke. It was just a joke. Listen, I'm sorry, OK? I didn't know it bothered you that much. Wouldn't bother me if I had a sister who looked like her. She's not a tart. She just looks like any girl her age, or any half-decent-looking one, anyway. God, the other day even my mum said what a nice girl she was turning into and how she wished my sister would be a bit more like Laura Patterson."

I swung round and blazed at him, ant-hot. "Yeah, well, you don't know anything. You haven't a clue what it's like, any of it." I turned away again, in case he saw how I bit my lip. "Anyway, it doesn't matter. Forget it," I mumbled. But I couldn't forget it. We went into the classroom together, but it wasn't the same. I had made everything different. Everything was dirty.

Dreeg rubbed his slimy hands. His eyes were turning slitty yellow again.

Why the hell did Laura have to be like that? I fizzed with anger. I had looked at other girls like that before and called them names, but it's different when it's your sister. Especially when your so-called best friend starts to fancy her. Much too close to home. It destroys something, something safe and sure. It was all her fault that everything was spoiling. What did anyone else know about her? She was my sister. I was the one who knew her, wasn't I?

Back home, after school, Dreeg was impatient for me to start my English homework. "Come on, come on, hurry up!" he nagged, shifting from foot to foot with impatience. His excitement was infectious. His eyes shone, his pupils now the color of burnished coal.

I tasted Halloween and forgot the sourness of my argument with Tom. Dreeg could make me forget anything. He could change in an instant and I could twist with him, a leaf in a storm.

"I don't know where to start."

"Start with the feeling. The idea. The cauldron. Throw in the ingredients, a victim, a reason, atmosphere, poison. Mix it, conjure it. Till it starts to grow into something more than you planned. Till it has a life of its own. Alive and real."

I brought the screen into focus, more easily than ever before. I was getting the hang of it. But what did I want to put there? If I wanted to create a frightening story, then I should start with what I knew. Start with what was in my head.

What was in my head was Laura. It seemed that when I thought of her, secret fears turned themselves into grotesque shadows and filthy tastes. And in these shadows I kept seeing that strange masked metal man, who waited in the deep darkness of a cave and whispered to himself. He seemed to be watching Laura. As if she was his victim. What was the reason, the masked man's motive? He whispered that she was dirty, a slut. It was what I felt, too. I swallowed the rush of saliva.

I focused on this masked man. Twisted my thoughts into fear. Wove them into something solid. Spun them till sparks flew.

My story started to grow. My just-for-homework story.

The metal man had been watching the girl for long enough. He knew where she went, how she walked, what she feared, had watched her sleeping, could enter her thoughts. Now he was almost ready to finish her. He knew that he would do it with fire. In the woods. Alone. Where no one would find her. Only the charred remains of her melted lilac fingernails would be uneaten by the birds. First he would catch her, frighten her, blindfold her with spiders' webs, imprison her. After that . . . Well, after that he would see.

I continued to write what I saw.

He didn't do it in the dark. Evil walks as well by daylight. This was a blistering day when the world had a headache. When brains were microwaved. A photograph with too much light, blindingly, seethingly bright. The metal man sucked the energy from everything he met as he glided hungrily toward the school that almost-final day. Friday. Roasted rabbit Friday. A bird dropped out of the sky, dead at his feet. He skewered it with a stick, pushed the stick into the ground. With his silver fingers he opened the bird's eyes and walked on. The bird stared and in the woods all the animals fell silent. Waiting for evil to pass. He pulled a spider from his mouth and dropped it on the ground, where it became a thousand spiders, which crawled fast into the trees and hid there. Waiting for him to return with her.

I did write more of the story but I didn't manage to finish it. I couldn't see the ending. Endings are always the difficult bit in a story, the bit that often goes out of control. What with physiotherapy and everything, Roach couldn't expect me to finish it. He should be pleased enough that I had done that much.

I had never enjoyed writing a story before. But now, I was feeling power. I was enjoying the feeling that I was controlling, manipulating the people who would read it. Roach and everyone. They would be frightened by my story, my thoughts in words. I would cast them in its spell. Having Laura as the victim added to my enjoyment. It was like bashing a pillow. Except that bashing a pillow never did anyone any harm.

That night I lay sweating in the summer dusk waiting for sleep, which wouldn't come. Dreeg's screwdriver eyes watched me from a corner. He shifted and opened his mouth, as though about to say something. And then grunted, as if he had decided not to say it but wanted me to know that there was something he was considering saying. Well, he would say it if he wanted to and I couldn't be bothered to ask.

I closed my eyes and tried to think of nothing. But it's not possible, and the more I tried, the more my nothing was something.

"Well?" asked Dreeg.

"Well what?"

"This shadow memory, this cold and empty space in your head. This Laura thing. Shall we get to the bottom of it, excavate it, drain it like a boil?"

"There's nothing there," I lied, my heart beginning to race.

"So there's no harm in looking, then. If there's nothing there we can just fill it in and plug the hole. And it'll shut me up, won't it? Besides, you're not going to sleep if I keep on nagging you."

That was certainly true.

"So, supposing I agreed—just to stop you nagging me— what would you do? How exactly do you plan to discover what it is that you want to find?"

"With hypnotism. I'd hypnotize you and get you to relax. That way you'll remember things that you thought you'd forgotten." Dreeg's voice was soft and human, friendly and straight, transparent and caramel-flavored. He sat on his doctory swivel chair and smiled. I saw that his eyes were now toffee brown, staring into mine like Grandpa's.

I've always wanted to be hypnotized but I should never

have trusted him to do it. Something soft in his voice made me.

"OK, but you won't find anything. So, what do I do?"

"Nothing. Just listen."

His voice was the sound of waves washing seashells and soaking the sand in my head. I sank down into my mattress until I couldn't feel it. I couldn't feel anything touching me at all, only a rushing of feathers in my veins, flitting and whispering, floating me fast down a tunnel.

Back down the volcano's throat I spun, past the purple wakening and into cotton-wool nothing. Hospital humming sounds and the smell of needles. Floating and a sense of being nowhere. Then further back, where everything was agony, sickness, shaking and fear. I was clawing at my head, trying to squash the spearing pain and tear it out. I was being rushed along a corridor and people were shouting. Someone was slapping my arm and something was pushed over my face despite my drowsy moaning.

Further back Dreeg's voice took me. To the smell of vomit and pine disinfectant and the cold tiled floor of the boys' toilets. Still a little way further back until I stopped and began to move forward again. And immediately everything became horribly clear, as Dreeg conducted my memory into words.

Going Back

I was stumbling toward the boys' toilets. Stumbling because the headache that had been brewing all day had become a seething red mess. I couldn't see properly, was squinting in the blinding light. One hand was over my eyes and the other was clutching my neck, both hands supporting my head. I knew I was going to throw up very soon. And it wasn't the first time that day. Black stars spun past my head as I rushed into the toilets and slumped against the wall just inside a cubicle. I pressed my forehead against the coolness of the wall and felt my limbs sink.

Graffiti covered the wall. I had read most of it before but now I read it again through fuzzy vision, trying to take my mind off the pain and the sickness. The cubicle was dark and relaxing. Among the usual stuff, something new. Something that might have been written in neon ink for all its glaringness. "Laura P will do it for free."

I vomited.

Then voices outside. Paul. And his gang. I pulled myself

up, flung open the door and staggered out. Saw the surprise on the faces, heard them laughing, felt the smack on his face as I hit him. Then they were on me, dragging me into a cubicle and forcing my head into the toilet. As water flushed over my face I heard Paul say, "Not as cute as his sister, but just as easy," and they all laughed as I collapsed toward blackness. Then the zigzag taste of confusion.

I half came round as the sirens rang and I was carried away on a stretcher, leaving their shocked faces behind. As the sick smell of disinfectant faded into the distance, I swam from the disgust and anger into blackness, until I came face to face with the present.

Dreeg was looking at me, his eyes now yellow, with thin black slits again. No longer smelling of caramel and trust. Snake's urine. I didn't want to know what he had shown me.

"So, that was it. Seems like a pretty good reason to hate your sister, if you ask me."

I was right about Laura, then. But I did not want to be right. I did not want a sister who flaunted herself like a slag, who slept around, who had boys talking and laughing about her, even had my best friend ogling her legs. At that moment, I really did wish harm on her. Wished it with all my power.

Tuesday. Tuesday was smooth apricot ice cream.

On the bus to school, Tom sat next to me as usual, but we didn't wrestle. Our sentences were tambourine-tight, discordant. I almost sent him a text message, but I didn't. I couldn't look at Laura, couldn't breathe when she passed.

Then Wednesday. Not an ordinary day. It was already hot

when I woke up. Some early mornings are such a hollow orange that you know they will boil. That was my first waking thought that Grandpa-apple Wednesday. The usual pale Wednesday color was overthrown by the glaring *W*, the color of uncooked beef, and the two *d*s a furious volcano red.

My second thought was more a shudder than a thought. A premonition, as it turned out.

The English lesson was when it happened.

First, though, there was the moment when Roach held up my story.

"And now we have the chilling story by Luke Patterson. This is marvelous, Luke. Super, just super. I shivered when I read it, positively shivered. For a moment I thought I could feel the presence of this man, this creature, this embodiment of evil. And there's so much you haven't told us, which is excellent—you are playing with your reader in a most wonderfully effective way. So many questions for us to wonder about: who is the girl, for example? What has she done wrong? Why does she go with this sinister man? Who is he? Is he imaginary? Is he real? Is he meant to represent something else? But you don't want to hear me going on, do you? You want to hear Luke's story, don't you?"

Mumbles from the class and a distinct lack of enthusiasm. But of course I was going to have to read it. I walked slowly and carefully to the front of the class, willing my leg to move smoothly.

And began to read.

The metal man without a face had been watching the girl for long enough. He knew where she went, how she walked, what she feared, had watched her sleeping, could enter her thoughts. Now he was ready to finish her. And he knew that he would do it with fire. In the woods. Alone. Where no one would find her. Only the charred remains of her melted lilac fingernails would be uneaten by the birds. First he would catch her, frighten her, blindfold her with spiders' webs, imprison her. After that . . . Well, after that he would see.

He didn't do it in the dark. Evil walks as well in daylight. This was a blistering day when the world had a headache. When brains were microwaved. A photograph with too much light, blindingly, seethingly bright. The metal man sucked the energy from everything he met as he glided hungrily toward the school that final day. Friday. Roasted rabbit Friday. A bird dropped out of the sky, dead at his feet. He skewered it with a stick, pushed the stick into the ground. With his silver fingers he opened the bird's eyes and walked on. The bird stared and in the woods all the animals fell silent. Waiting for evil to pass. He pulled a spider from his mouth and dropped it on the ground, where it became a thousand spiders, which crawled fast into the trees and hid there. Waiting for him to return with her.

The man had no clothes but he was not naked. He had no shape, no angles. Was smooth in black silver, without seams or pockets. Sprayed on. On his head, no nose, no hair. No face, but a mask, black holes where eyes would be, a mouth closed, yet grinning. A body wrapped in flowing mercury. Voodoo drumbeats from faraway, a dancing medicine man chanting curses in the forest, the smell of frightened cats.

At the edge of the woods, he stood outside the school and watched. He called out in a whisper. "You! Come here, little slut! Unclean, dirty slag!" But only the deaf girl heard. She looked out the window and smiled coolly at the man with the metal face. He slowly raised his hand and pointed. "Her!" he whispered. The deaf girl stood up and tapped the victim on the *shoulder. The victim turned to the window, her black eyes wide and empty. She knew and she did not know. Smelt it on the heavy air. Felt it in the breath of the man as it reached her with the taste of smoke. Heard it in the crackle of flames, in the screams of a frying hedgehog. She gasped with fear but still walked out the door toward him.*

Suddenly, there was a scream.

Losing Control

It **was Ishbel**, a wispy girl who always looked as though she would float away if you sneezed on her. She was pointing at the girl next to her. Carla's desk faced the window. She was trying to get out of her chair, pushing her desk back with a scraping screech, shouting, "No! I'm going to faint! I'm going to faint!" The skin on her face was stretched tight and colorless, her eyes were squashed and her lips were snarled back like a mad dog's. Her head was shaking from side to side. Suddenly, her eyes opened and the whites rolled up into her head as she fell to the floor, where she lay jerking. Her tongue was stuck out, clenched between her teeth.

The classroom door banged shut, but as far as I saw no one had left. Everyone was looking at Carla. No one else looked out the window, but I did. As I peered into the blinding glare I was sure I saw a figure at the edge of the woods, looking up at the school. A flock of birds flew up into the air and when I looked harder the figure had gone. The long grass was moving as though someone was passing through.

A smell of burning again, or was it just the sun scorching my desk? I shivered. This was the snakeskin smell of fear. I felt it in my stomach, vomit-sharp.

By this time, Roach had taken control. He had sent someone to get the school secretary and had told us all to stand back. "What do you normally do when Carla does this?" he asked us.

"She's never done it before," said someone.

"What's wrong with her?" asked someone else.

"It's an epileptic fit," said Will. Will is not a friend of mine. No special reason. Will's parents are both university lecturers, which means that his school projects are always absurdly impressive. He knows everything about everything and speaks with such confidence that even if you think he's talking rubbish, somehow you can't say so. He is a grown-up already.

A couple of girls were crying. Several people were looking at me suspiciously.

"It's all Luke's fault," said Will, "with that stupid story."

"Don't be silly, William," said Roach. "It's nothing to do with the story. It was a marvelous story. When Luke has finished writing the end, I think we'll all want to hear it."

"I don't want to hear it," said Ishbel. "It gave me the creeps."

"Look at Daniel," laughed Will. "He's gone funny, too."

We all looked. Daniel was standing at the window, staring out, white-faced, shaking and pointing, trying to speak but with no sound coming from his mouth. Jostling each other for a position near the window, we followed the direction of his pointing finger. I saw the figure first because I knew where to look and what to look for. Someone breathed, "Oh my God!" and there were gasps.

I focused the screen in front of me and blanked it out white, airbrushed it all out with a breath, as fast as I could. "There's nothing there," I said quickly. "Nothing at all. It was just my made-up story."

"I can't see anything, either," said someone. "Nor can I," echoed some others, relieved. Tom said nothing but stared at me, and I could see the cogs in his brain spinning behind his glass face.

"Well, I saw someone," said Will. "A man with a metal mask, all creepy and spooky and coming to get *you!*" and he made a monster face toward us.

"Shut up!" I said angrily, frantic for it all not to be true. "I just hypnotized you, that's all. You just imagined it because of my story. It's called autosuggestion. Haven't you heard of that, Will?"

"Settle down now, everyone," shouted Roach, as Miss Edwards, the school secretary, came in. By this time Carla had recovered from whatever it was and was sitting looking dopey. Miss Edwards took her out.

"Weirdo," said Will as he passed me on his way back to his seat.

"Zombie," whispered Mike.

"Mutant," muttered Zahra.

"Psycho," said Colin.

"I saw him," said Daniel.

"Be quiet, Daniel," said Roach unsympathetically.

"We are not in the middle of the Gobi Desert, you know. People do walk along that road. It was just, as Luke so rightly pointed out, autosuggestion."

"Suck up," whispered Will. Tom was silent.

Dreeg leaned forward and whispered weevils in my ear. "Like clockwork, Luke. Going like clockwork. Beautiful control, just beautiful. Couldn't have done it better myself. But do you know where it's going, that's the question? Have you got a plan?"

No, I did not have a plan. In fact, now I did not feel in control at all. I had started writing a story, just any old homework story. But now there was a man, a creature who had started in my head uninvited, but whom other people could now see, or so it seemed. You would think that I shouldn't be afraid of something I had made. That I could make it go away. But I didn't know what or where it was. It had a power of its own, an element of future chaos, like everything that happened in my head.

I tried to say all this to Dreeg. But he only smiled and said, "Well, Luke, if you are not in control of your own mind, who is?"

The snake of fear flickered its tongue deep inside me. Almost fully grown now, it rhythmically pushed, until its old skin was shed and it emerged into its new form, glistening and strong. I began to realize what I was frightened of. I began to wish that this was all a bad dream and that I would wake up soon. I began to wish I was someone else, because surely if I had been different, done things differently, none of this would be happening?

Means and Ends

Athletics that evening helped me take my mind off the incident in the classroom. I knelt by the track with Tom as we put our running shoes on together, as we always had, but not as we always had.

In my head I was tossed by all the conflicting things I wanted to say to him. That I was angry. That something was making me this way. That I wished it would all go away. That I was sorry. I wanted to tell him about how everything had changed, even about the flying.

"You can't tell him," said Dreeg. "He's ordinary. He wouldn't understand. He's weak. And maybe he's not such a good friend after all. Look at the way he looks at Laura."

Music tastes of bat's pee.

Mr. Breslin called Tom to go and practice sprint starts. "See ya," Tom said quietly as he stood up. By the time I looked up, he was walking away from me.

I ran badly to start with. I couldn't tell anyone that I still felt weak. Dreeg was jumping up and down. He was marshmallow-scented slime, running through my fingers, impossible to catch. Changing shape so often that it was confusing. He mirrored the chaos inside my own head.

"Use it, Luke! Use your power!"

"It's cheating. I can fly if I want to. But they can't." I wanted him to help me justify it.

"I'm not asking you to fly. Just run fast and strong."

"I can't run fast and strong without cheating."

"It's not cheating. It's your power. If someone had the power of running faster than anyone else in the world, would you say he shouldn't use that power, just because it meant he would surely win?"

"This isn't the same. This isn't natural. This is the same as taking drugs—a pill for running like the wind. If there was a pill like that it would be illegal."

"It's nothing like taking a pill, you pathetic boy. It's using your mind. That's what top athletes do all the time and it's not illegal. It's called visualization. They visualize themselves winning, or scoring or whatever, and lo and behold! They do win."

"Yes, but if they visualize themselves flying, they don't fly, do they?"

"Maybe they could if they were good enough at visualizing."

"I don't think so, somehow."

"Well, can't you at least visualize your leg running strongly? Not magically strong, not flying strong. Just as strong as it was before you were ill? That wouldn't be too much to ask, would it? I mean, can I first please make it absolutely clear that this running business matters nothing to me? It's just that I want to show you what you can have. All you want."

So I looked inside, grasped a golden apple, and won the next race. Simple, but not simple.

"See?" said Dreeg. "That wasn't too hard, was it?"

"That's the problem. It's not hard. I can do anything, remember?" I snapped. Stuck. Fly-in-jam stuck.

"You want to win, don't you? You know the feeling of winning? Do you know the feeling of losing, Luke?" No, but it smelt of rats eating a fox corpse. Dead black. "You'll do what it takes to win, won't you, Luke? Wish your leg strong, tell them it was a miracle, tell them you trained like hell—I don't care what you say. I don't care if you win, anyway. But I know you'll do what it takes. Any other way, you'll lose. Lose everything. And I don't want that to happen."

I closed my mind to the demonic crawling face before me, held my breath against the stench of guilt, and vowed to win at all costs. Work out the excuses later.

In the end, I needn't have bothered, for reasons that will become clear, and it all goes back to the poem and my sister Laura finding it. You see, she hadn't forgotten.

Not quite yet, though. First, Thursday. Under the dead blue deep of Thursday, only weird lunar creatures can survive. The rest of us just wilt, unable to breathe, like being underwater and not knowing which way is up. The veins stick out on our feet and hands like umbilical cords and it seems as if they will burst at any moment.

Dad is stretched with worry. He chews the sides of his fingers as he watches his mobile phone, waiting for a fire that he knows must come. Needing it, so that he can act.

Sure enough, on the news, a forest fire in a nearby wood,

but not ours. A dog goes mad in the heat and savages a small child. A boy dies from shock after jumping into a cold pool. A two-headed snake is seen by a family on a walking holiday. And a teenage girl is attacked somewhere, some miles away, far enough. She is found gibbering and wrecked, half her clothes burnt away and her feet blistered, too frightened to tell what happened. Or who took her. The papers don't say what her gibbering consists of, but police warn young women not to go out alone.

Laura's clothes now became smaller in the heat, covering less. There were more wasps in her hair and the sweat on her upper lip smelt of the juice of a ham. I wanted to close her mouth with plasticine and plug her nostrils with frog spawn. It was obvious how she loved her long smooth legs and the way her careless skirt rode up too far when she sat down.

In the lunch break, Tom and I were silently kicking a ball. It was what we always did, so not doing it would have been an admission that there was something wrong. Eyes do not meet when you kick a ball. We could almost pretend that everything was normal.

We both ran for the ball, but it bounced against a stone and rolled round the corner. I reached the corner first. I stopped. Tom reached the ball but stopped when he saw what I had seen. Just there, right in front of us, less than five meters away, were Laura and Paul, kissing deeply. Paul's hands were at the tiny edge of her skirt. They looked absurd, like child actors learning their parts. And disgusting, tasting each other like that. I wished Tom had not seen.

Paul looked toward me and stuck a finger in the air at me. I lunged.

The Ugly Truth

Tom pulled me back. "Ignore them, Luke. They're not worth it."

"She's an embarrassment. Look at her sticky slug-lips. Look at her slut's legs. She makes me puke. Let's get them. Let's get her and her slimy git boyfriend." My fingers were pressing into the palms of my hands. The ugly taste of graffiti on green toilet walls.

Tom let go my arm and drew back. "What's got into you, Luke? You're acting weird these days. She's just a girl and he's just a creep. What do you want? To beat him up? Count me out. I don't do that stuff and nor do you. Or so I thought. I've totally had enough. Christ's sake, get your act together." He walked away toward our other friends and I was left alone. I wanted to call him back, explain things properly. But I was earthquake angry.

"Leave him," said Dreeg softly in my ear. "He doesn't understand. You are right to be angry with Laura. She deserves it. You are on the side of right. You'll see that soon. Everyone will see that soon, then your so-called friend will be sorry he didn't support you."

He may have been in my head but it felt as though his arm was around my shoulders. Supporting me, understanding. I had no one else to turn to. I went with him and left Tom. A blue taste. The squeaky sound of too-thin ice.

Friday. Chocolate-sticky roasting Friday. Shit-brown slimy throat-clogging mud-drowning Friday. The day when Laura got her revenge.

I was already on the bus when I saw Tom get on, not glance at me, and sit two rows in front. I closed my eyes. At school, he got off without waiting. Everything was shriveling at the edges.

Friday was the day of the school newsletter. That was true of every last Friday of a month and this was the last Friday in June.

It was one thing to have my frighten-the-life-out-of-them story read out in class. But a different thing altogether to have a love poem, mine, printed in the school newsletter, posted on every notice board and distributed to every pupil to take home to admiring parents. She'd even given it a title: "My First Love" by Luke Patterson. She'd decorated it with chubby hearts and there was a little sketch of me going down on one knee, with a soppy expression on my face and a bunch of black tulips in my hands.

The news spread like arson around the school. "Have you seen the poem by Luke Patterson? He sent it in for the newsletter! What's he on? Sicko. He's in lurv." Wet-dream weirdo was one of the things they called me.

Even my friends laughed. Tom, too. Anyone would. I mean, people like me just don't write things like that. And if they do, they certainly don't volunteer them for the school newsletter. Only dags, saddos, do things like that.

I burned, spat inside with fury. Dreeg seeped pus from every pore, stank of sewers. Everything in front of my eyes was ugly, buzzing with filth. I thought I would vomit. I saw Laura at the end of a corridor. Over her shoulder I saw the metal man watching her and I pointed at him. Laura turned but saw only Paul walking toward her. She smiled as she went to Paul and they locked themselves together.

Paul looked over Laura's shoulder and his black eyes smiled at me. I heard him breathe, saw drops of silver blood slowly drip from his nostrils. His face was merging into itself like mercury and I saw his thoughts. "I've got the slag. She's mine." A white spider crawled out of his fingers and up Laura's back and neck. It buried itself in her hair. Softly, Paul blew, and her hair caught fire, as the wasps flew shrieking from it and disappeared angrily toward the woods.

My insides rotted as the man with the metal mask breathed fast. He had a box of huge matches in one hand and a dead bird in the other. As I watched him, a hedgehog burst into flames at his feet and I smelt roasting flesh.

I wished her dead. The ugly truth. Just momentarily.

That was the moment. A moment of revelation when I could have saved myself. A part of me that was my old self, my old, ordinary, fantastically ditchwater-ordinary self, caught a glimpse of what I had become. I saw the stench of what I had thought: I had wanted my sister dead. What was I, that I could be like that? Nothing was worth the horror of it—not flying, not power, not running, not winning, not anything that I could think of. I would fly once more and tell Dreeg that this was it. I would give it up this time. I would resist all the temptation of power.

I ran from the school, dragging my sullen leg, toward the woods. I don't know if anyone saw me go but no one followed. Through the long grass, I ran through the heat toward the darkness. Silence hung over the woods, as if everything was holding its breath, waiting to see what I would do.

"I'm saying no, Dreeg. I'll prove it. I want to fly!" I screamed. "Right now, one last time. Because I don't want any of this. I don't want this power. I don't care whether I can hold the universe in my hand. I don't even care about running, or winning. I'll lose for the rest of my life if that's what happens. I'll prove it, you creep. Come on, then, let's fly!"

Dreeg just smiled. "Very well, Luke, let's go. That's just fine by me. Your little twinge of guilt is pathetic, by the way. Let's go, then. What are you waiting for?"

I turned my brain inside out and focused on the screen. Sucked lemonade ice through my veins and flew, high, fast and swooping. Yelled an eagle and sang pink bubblegum. Spun in the space between the stars. Dived down toward an ocean and sent the smoothest, whitest stone skim-skim-skimming, hopping three thousand times across the trampoline skin of the water.

"Say it, Luke. Say you don't want it. That you want to go back to normal now. Run the race on your own and lose with your lead-weight leg? Be dull again? Ditchwater dull? Brain-damaged, not brain-different."

"You can't tempt me. Get out, Dreeg! I hate what you have shown me, what you are doing to me, what you have made me. I can be better than this without you."

"You don't mind losing? Loser!"

"Go! Now!" I screamed. And he smiled.

Seraphina

"**A** re you sure?** Look first." And he pointed down, the devil in his eyes, eyes that were now a forked red.

I couldn't help it, I looked down in the direction he was pointing, saw the school below as I swooped and floated. Saw a girl walking through the buttery heat toward the entrance. She walked into the building and I tasted cinnamon.

"Seraphina, Luke. What happens to Seraphina if you throw all this away? Will she disappear?"

"She can't just disappear. She's walked into the school. She's there. She can't just suddenly be un-there, whatever you think you might do about it."

"She can disappear. She appeared, didn't she? Depends how real she is. You don't know, do you? Admit it—you just don't know."

I breathed a wish, tried to grasp the structure of a smoke-cell. I didn't know.

"Can you risk it? Risk her not being real? Risk her disappearing? And everything else."

—

I walked into the school shortly after her. I did not look at Dreeg. But I knew that he was gorging himself on my soul. Looking back now, after all that happened later, I despise my weakness at that moment. Dreeg had a hold on me that I could not break, because he was a part of me. It seemed then quite possible that I would never be free of him, that I would have to learn to live with him.

Are you wondering how I could have been so weak? How so soon after vowing to turn my back on all this craziness, I gave in to temptation? I can only say that there was something about Seraphina that called out to me. I created her, after all. She was a part of me, just like Dreeg, and it was clear that I could not have one without the other.

She was waiting for me inside the building. Everyone else streamed past us on the way to lessons, but I noticed no faces.

When Seraphina smiled at me, I tasted vanilla sugar. Her thickened voice was not what I expected. It enveloped me and held me close. She knew my name and, just like a dream, it seemed quite reasonable that she should.

"Hi, Luke. . . . I'll maybe see you after school? What are you doing?" Just like that. I felt the whisper of her eyes on my mouth as she read my reply.

"Athletics. Come to training—you have to. I've seen you run. You—"

"OK," and when she opened her mouth wide to say "OK," candy-floss bubbles floated away. I breathed in the honeyed warmth of her hair.

"See you later." She waved as she disappeared down the

corridor. I called her name, but of course she didn't hear. I went back to my classroom, drugged by her scent.

Struggling through the dull heat of lessons, I began to feel ill. I thought the day would never end. Voices barely penetrated a growing muffled ache in my head. I could not draw a full breath—each one stuck as though a horse was sitting on my chest.

Without Seraphina's presence, I was left with Dreeg and the memory of what I had done. I throbbed with the effort of ignoring his smugness. I did not look at him.

I couldn't look at Tom, either. He kept his head down in class and our eyes never met. I looked at no one, blocked them all out. Blocked out what I had done.

Seraphina was on the bus with me. The fact that I tasted cinnamon when I looked at her and that every now and then butterflies flittered from her eyes was something I had come to expect by now from my muddled senses. I had to admit that it added extra sides to ordinary feelings, turned dull moments into fairground rides with surprises round every corner.

Dreeg was quiet, breathing at the edge of my mind. Asleep? Waiting. Suspiciously silent. Like a storm that is drawing breath, sucking everything in before exploding it out.

The metal man was nowhere to be seen but the heat was growing and the sweat dripped from us all. The air was a pond.

At athletics training later that evening, I was putting my shoes on, sitting on my own as though I didn't mind, when I saw Seraphina come toward me. Her smile lifted me. But I also thought she was looking at me more intently, with a tiny question in her eyebrows.

I didn't find out what it was until halfway through athletics, when we were waiting for our next run.

By the way, she ran like a dream. Flipped my insides right over to watch her unnatural speed.

I, on the other hand, ran like a nightmare. Saving myself, I said. The truth was—well, there were several truths. One was that I had a pulsing sick headache tinged with fear. Was this meningitis again? Another was that it was too hot to run. I could even claim that my focus had been damaged by the stresses of the day. Post-traumatic stress disorder. But really, it was that Dreeg did not offer his help and I couldn't bring myself to ask for it, after what had happened. The heat of the day sapped my strength. He sat reeking in his sleep and I wanted him to stay there. I assumed I would need him when the time came to race for real, but just now I really couldn't face him and his arrogance. And the fact that he had won. Sounds feeble, I know. But I was tired.

Very tired. More than tired. A head pain deep and blinding. My neck ached and I wanted to shut my eyes. I felt sick. A dark memory of having been here before. A growing fear and an ache in my bad leg.

Anyway, I found out what Seraphina was thinking.

"I've got a confession," she said. Her voice moves slowly through apple sauce. She puts more effort into her words than other people. They come from deeper inside.

I looked at her through headache eyes.

"I read it."

"Read what?" and as I asked, I knew.

"Read your poem."

Synesthesia

Then **I** thought I really would throw up. I swayed. Her smile was orange. "How do you do it?" she asked.

"Do what?"

"Write like that. When I read it I saw the girl. I mean really saw her, smelt, tasted. All just as you said."

I couldn't breathe. Stung with sweat. Didn't know what to say. Did she know that the girl was her? And even if she did not, didn't she think it was pathetic, sick-bucket soppy?

"There's something else," she said. I was paralyzed. My head swam.

"You said—I remember exactly—'feel the sounds of strawberries on my fingers.' What do you mean when you say that?"

"Oh, it's nothing, just stuff, just poem-language stuff. The sort of stuff English teachers like. It doesn't mean anything at all."

"It does to me. It describes exactly, perfectly, what happens in my head. Only, I can never seem to write it down in a way that works. Sounds of strawberries. When I smell a strawberry, I hear it. As if I wasn't deaf. I thought maybe you did, too. I thought maybe you had it, too."

She looked away, a pink sweat on her forehead and a tiny ladybird on her ear.

"Had what?" I asked. She didn't hear. She was turned away. I touched her arm. The music of banana purée. She looked at my mouth. "Had what?" I repeated.

She paused. "Synesthesia." A swish of sand.

"What?" I'd never heard the word but it sounded like hope.

"Synesthesia. It's a condition where the senses are muddled. When you touch something, you might experience it in color, or as a smell, kind of feeling a color. I can't explain. Music can taste of anything from—"

"Banana purée to bat's pee," I said.

Seraphina smiled. "You do!" she said. "You do have it! I knew you must!"

"I didn't know it had a name. I didn't even know anyone else had it."

"You mean you've gone your whole life thinking you were the only one?"

"I didn't have it before. I was ill. Meningitis. I nearly died. And when I woke up I had this thing, this syn-whatever-you-call-it." I hesitated. "And can you . . . use it?"

"What do you mean?"

"Can you use it, this way of seeing things? Can you change things?"

Seraphina looked blank. "Like?"

"Nothing, I was just thinking." But I really did need to

know if she could change things, if she had a Dreeg creature in her head, too. God, but I wished she had, so I needn't be alone and weird. "Like when you said you could see the girl I wrote about. The imaginary girl," I added quickly.

"Well, yes, I could see her. That's because of the way you wrote it."

"But was she there?"

"Yes, I suppose she was. I don't know. I've forgotten. I thought it was because I do see things like that when people describe them."

"Can you do it, though? Make people see things that aren't there? Make things happen? Create things? Could you make something with your words?"

"No, I don't think so. I've never tried. What are you saying, Luke?"

Just then my head burst into flames inside. White missiles zagged across my vision and the pain swelled to a scream. I fell back on the ground with glaring voices holding me. My neck was locked in a vise and I burnt all over. Vomit rose in my throat. In a spark I had time for one crazed thought: meningitis. I was going to die and there was nothing I could do about it. I plunged into the watery spinning darkness and gave up.

The Worm Turns

I woke in an ambulance. Or partly woke, and curled back into my hot yellow hole again. A knife scraped at the back of my eyeballs and lemon-juice violin screams seeped into the scratches. I walked on an ocean of sand. And the sand dived away beneath my feet, as I dropped into nowhere again.

Although I was not there, I heard the sirens from a long way away. Every time a bomb dropped, my eyes exploded magnesium again. A tangle of noise clattered beneath me and shook me in its fist.

Soon it was quieter. I was moved by strong hands. Entered by pins. Flooded with liquids and soothed by cool breath. All in a darkened cotton-wool milky place with muffled smells the shape of circles. I blew bubbles like a fish. I knew I had died but the terror was somewhere else, outside.

Many eons later I woke properly. In hospital. White sheets. Mum and Dad again, just like the first time. No

Laura, though. No wasps. But Dreeg watching from a corner. I closed my eyes, but he was still there, tapping his claws impatiently. His hands, which once had been soft as they stroked the inside of my brain, were now hard, taloned, like an animal's. Almost hoofed.

It is not easy to describe what I was feeling. Something like hanging from an airplane on a thin rope. Paralyzed. A tiny fly in a web. Was it meningitis again? How long had I been in a coma this time? Would everything have changed again?

I tried to speak but my lips were glued and dry and no sound came out. Mum held my head and dripped some water into my mouth. She wiped my face with something damp and I wished I could stay here forever. I was safe here.

"Shhh, Luke," she whispered. "No need to talk." I loved the way her blond hair shone, streaked by the sun. I always smelt strawberries when Mum whispered.

"But what happened?" I had to know.

"You got too hot, that's all. Heatstroke and probably a migraine, the doctor says. You were at athletics, remember? I knew I shouldn't have let you go."

"Not meningitis, then?"

"No, not meningitis," said Dad. I somersaulted inside myself. "But that's what everyone thought. That's why the ambulance. That's why Mum called me. But there's nothing to worry about. You'll be right as rain. Don't even have to stay in for the night."

"I feel as if I've been here for ages. What day is it?"

"Still Friday," Dad said, smiling. "Seven o'clock. You fainted and then you slept. That's all. You hungry?"

"Don't be silly," said Mum. "Course he's not hungry. He's got heatstroke." She seemed to love the sound of the word. Heatstroke. So much less terrifying than meningitis. Stroked by the heat, not eaten away by lethal bacteria.

She was right. I wasn't hungry. Because when Dad said the word *Friday*, sweet chocolate flooded in and Dreeg squelched his now toadsome body toward me with a grin. I closed my eyes and watched the shape of voodoo drumbeats behind my eyes.

"Back, then, Luke, are we? How delightful."

"Go away. I'm tired," I muttered in my head.

"Tired of what? You haven't done anything. You didn't run properly. You didn't use your power. You didn't even ask me for help. What is going on, Luke? Lost your will to win?"

"Maybe."

"Oh well, never mind. Who cares? As you must know by now, I couldn't give a damn whether you win or lose your pathetic little race, Luke. It means nothing to me. I never have understood the point. But this power of yours, now, that's a different matter altogether. That I do care about. Most certainly I do. And it means everything to me that you should learn to use it. Choose to use it. Grow it. Like a beanstalk with all the gold in the world at the end of it."

"Why? What is it to you? What do you get out of this, anyway?" He was making my headache worse.

Dreeg smiled. "You may not want to change the world, Luke. But I do. Oh yes. I certainly do. Want to change it most definitely. Most dramatically. The world needs to be changed. It is ripe for changing."

"So why don't you just go and do it, then? You're obviously so bloody powerful—just go and change the flaming world and leave me out of it. Why do you need me?"

Dreeg seethed as he shifted uncomfortably. Green acid bubbled from the marsh of his skin.

"That would be telling, Luke. And I am not telling you. Certainly not."

I sensed something in his voice. Could it be fear? The thought that Dreeg might be afraid and that there was something he didn't want me to know—now, that was very interesting indeed. But I was too tired to grasp the thought properly and I let it go. I would come back to it later.

Just then a doctor came to my bed. "Well, young man. Been overdoing it a bit, have we? All this running in the heat. Now, let's see. Hmmm." He buried himself in my notes, as if they were going to tell him something interesting. "Weekend taking it easy, and you'll be right as rain by Monday. If only it would—rain, I mean—don't you think?" he said, turning to Mum and Dad.

"There's bound to be thunder soon. Good storm, that's what everyone needs," said Dad. "Clear the air. Damp down the vegetation, otherwise there's a serious risk of a major fire. I've been worried about it for days. No rain for weeks and everything dry as tinder." A muscle at the side of his face flickered and his hand went to his mobile phone for reassurance.

"Well, let's hope not," said the doctor, turning to Mum. "Anyway. You can take him home now. Keep him quiet over the weekend. Make sure he drinks lots—not fizzy drinks, though. Let us know if you're worried about anything. And stay out of the sun, young man," he said, turning to me.

"Stay cool, as you young people would say." He winked at me as if using the word *cool* made him one of me. I couldn't manage a smile back. To tell the truth, my brain still felt crunched. Scraping metal fingernails.

There were smooth blue insects in the wrinkles of his face. He turned away and moved on to the next patient.

We gathered my things together and left the observation ward. Driving home, I closed my eyes and tried to let it all wash away.

As we approached our house, we could see Laura sitting on the doorstep. She leapt up when she saw us and yelled, "Where the bloody hell have you been? I've been sitting here for three-quarters of an hour!"

Mum scrambled to apologize. "Oh, I'm so sorry, Laura, but we got a call saying Luke had been taken to the hospital again and I didn't—"

"Oh, how tragic! Well, if Lukey had to go to the hospital, then that's quite all right, of course. Obviously nothing too serious. I'm *so* glad. What about me? I'm going out in half an hour and look at me."

"Do we have to?" I asked.

"Oh, why don't you just f—"

"Laura! That's enough! We're back now. Let's just get in the door, can we?"

"I was only going to say, 'Why don't you just find yourself a mirror and make yourself throw up?' "

Amber was barking by now from inside the house. "Excuse me, Laura," I said. "You're not the only dog in my life, you know." And I followed Mum into the house.

"Cripple," Laura muttered under her breath.

I was going to continue the war of words but Dreeg whispered in my ear. "Leave her, Luke. She'll keep."

Later, I sat in the shade at the side of the house, the only cool place Mum could find. She put a bowl of water on the ground and I rested my bare feet in it. A bottle of water stood near me and Mum gave me instructions to drink it slowly. Its coldness slipped down my throat. I waited for my head to cool.

Seraphina came by, her smile warm as plums. As she walked toward me, an image flashed into my head without warning. Through the computer screen, I saw her running like a deer through the trees, faster than the flames that chased her. The metal man raised his arm. In it crouched a knife. The metal man held the knife near his empty eye socket and followed the deer with a smile. He drew his arm back slowly and slashed it forward. A whistle as the steel shattered the air like glass and the deer fell stone cold on the forest floor. Dreeg laughed from a distance, and I smelt blue ice as my heart stopped.

But suddenly Seraphina was there beside me and she sat down. I inhaled the realness of her and pushed the image away. It was just a symptom of my illness, I decided. I tried to remind myself that the metal man was a figment of my imagination and my story, and that his imaginary victim was Laura.

Seraphina looked so strong, as though she could run faster than anything, faster surely than flames and knives. They do in films, don't they? Heroes and heroines? They outrun the rolling fireball, the sliding lava, the bursting flood, the hail of arrows.

Dreeg was licking his lips, dribbling. Fat as a walrus. Ugly as evil.

"You can have her if you want," he said.

"She's not yours to give," I replied. "She's herself." There was a new coolness in my voice, more anger than fear, and a resolution to use him more than he could use me.

Dreeg snarled quietly, as if reading my thoughts. I focused on his tongue, pulling it out of his mouth. It came like an endless worm, covered in ulcers. I pulled it and wrapped it four times around his neck and laughed. Now, that was a power worth having.

Suddenly Dreeg lashed out, stinging my brain with an octopus arm. A thousand electric needles.

War

I winced. Seraphina turned to me. "Are you all right?" The concern in her voice was real.

"Yes, fine. Just pins and needles," I lied. "Sorry, I'm not up to talking much, but please stay."

"Don't worry. Close your eyes. I'll sit here."

Dreeg glared cobra eyes at me. "Just watch yourself, Luke," he said. "Don't mess around with me. My patience is not endless, you know. You need me. Need me sweet." Green treacle dripped from his lips onto my eyelids and seeped into me, hypnotizing. "Need me on your side. You want to win and you want Seraphina. I may not understand why, but I am the only one who knows how much you want those two things. And unfortunately for you, without me you can guarantee neither. So knuckle under, young man, and understand that winning carries a price. The price is that you do as I say. Got it?"

Words swirled around my head but I didn't speak them.

He continued. "Remember what I have done for you.

What I have given you. The world I have shown you. The passion I have opened up for you. I have flown through the stars with you. I have shown you how you can conquer any weakness to win. Through you, I have turned reeking water into the sweetest lemonade and led you to drink. I have shown you how to do these things yourself, to be like a god. I have given you power over others, shown you how to turn their minds. I even brought Seraphina to you. And you have not shown me any gratitude, Luke. Not once have you shown me gratitude or respect. You have not repaid me for what I have given you. You owe me. Oh yes, you owe me."

"I didn't ask for any of it."

"When you are given a present you didn't ask for, does that mean you refuse to say thank you?"

"No," I mumbled.

"So, what do you say?" Dreeg's eyes gleamed. "Go on— what do you say? What do you say?"

"Thank you," I said, with a degree of sullenness I could not quite hide.

For a moment Dreeg's eyes blazed with greed and fury, but the instant vanished. His voice softened, oozing sweet-mallow syrup. He stroked my thoughts. "I am too hard on you," he whispered through lips crusted with sugar. "You are only a boy. How can you understand and appreciate what I have done for you? Think nothing of it, Luke, my boy." He shrugged, throwing off his anger. "So, anyway, how are we going to get you fit for your race? Next weekend, isn't it? Quite a bit of work to do, wouldn't you say?"

"I thought you didn't care about my race. About whether I win or lose."

"But *you* care. And I am here to help *you*. Trust me." I don't know whether I really trusted him—it would be hard to imagine that I could have done after everything that had happened. But perhaps I just did what I had done all along: believed what I wanted to believe. Also, of course, Seraphina was there, and wasn't she there because I had told Dreeg to stay?

Seraphina didn't stay long. We talked awhile, but my head hurt. She could tell—I don't know, perhaps being deaf made her more tuned in to other things, like thoughts and feelings. Anyway, soon she went away and I closed my eyes against the empty place she had left in my head.

When I went up to my bed early—Mum's orders and I wasn't arguing—I heard Laura storming around her bedroom trying to get ready to go out. Dreeg grinned. "Let's have some fun, shall we, Luke? Just a bit of harmless fun."

"Like?"

"Just a game. Some minor tricks on Laura. Serve her right, wouldn't you say? Don't forget what she did to you today. That newsletter trick." I hadn't forgotten. I still fizzed at the thought of it. I did want to pay her back, but I definitely didn't mean I wanted her dead. In view of what happened later, it's important to make it clear that I did not mean I wanted her dead. That was just a momentary thing before, thought in anger, and it had shocked me. I just wanted to do something fitting, revenge for what she did to me. Ordinary brother-and-sister stuff. Something to make me feel better. It's just that it didn't work out like that. After all, I wasn't ordinary.

"Come on, let's do it. It will be fun," he urged.

"What do you have in mind?"

The Calm
Before the Storm

"No, it's what *you* have in *your* mind that's important. Use some imagination. Surely you can think of something?" Dreeg asked.

I heard the bathroom door close as Laura went for a shower. I brought the screen into focus, pulled an image from near the edge and massaged it with words, zapped it with the power of my language. A scream came from the shower as the water turned to ice.

A volcano in my head, another scream as the lava scorched her flesh. "Someone's using a tap!" she yelled. "Mum! Tell Luke to stop using the tap!"

As I walked past her bedroom, I sent an earthquake wind rushing around my brain. Jumbled purple noise. Ants scrambling in terror as their hill crumbled underfoot. And later as I lay on cool sheets, I heard her cursing as she found her spilt nail varnish and could not find a shoe.

It was nothing but an amusing interval. It meant nothing, really, in the grand scheme of things. Did not change the world in any way you would notice. But Dreeg seemed to enjoy it and I admit that it was a calming end to a violent day. A lighthearted moment.

Soon, as she went downstairs, I smelt her pass my room in cheap pink clothes. And heard, but still refused to understand fully, the breathing of the metal man in the darkness of my mind. Dreeg stroked my brain to sleep with a long bony talon, as though he cared deeply about my health and strength.

Seraphina came to see me again the next day, Saturday. We lay on our stomachs on the grass in the shade of a tree behind the house and exchanged the outlines of our lives. She was as different from Laura as it is possible for a girl to be. I didn't dare touch her. Seraphina was not the type of girl you touched so soon after meeting. Inhaling the sound of her was enough. A touch, a kiss, would have changed everything.

Normally, Tom would have come on a Saturday. We would have kicked a ball or walked down to the river and talked familiar nothings. I sent him a text message, "hi! u ok?" He didn't send one back.

A breeze took the sting out of the sun, and the summer holidays seemed closer. Laura was away most of the day, shopping or whatever. The house was a tiny boat on a calm sea.

On Sunday, I went with Seraphina to the river and we fished with homemade lines. I caught a tiny, ugly fish. At least, that's what I knew it was, but I made her think it was a monstrous pike with muscled fins and evil teeth. She was astonished that I chose to throw it back with a whirlpool splash, instead of taking it home to show the world what incredible creatures live in the River Ouse.

Later that evening, we went to the woods. In the cool of the setting sun, the shadows lengthened, making us look like giants. We acted the parts of stilt-walkers with long spider arms and chased each other. The woods held an eerie peace. They are rooted in stories of ancient wars and we were running over graves. Ogden, our maths teacher, told us once that every breath a person takes contains a tiny particle of Caesar's dying breath. I don't really believe it. But in these woods, the dying breaths of countless soldiers haunt the silence.

After the black heat of the day, the coolness of the trees gave me fresh energy.

"Let's race!" I said.

"Do you think you should?" asked Seraphina.

"Chicken! You just don't want to lose!" I taunted. "Race you to the corner?" It was about two hundred meters away, not my distance, but I could do anything.

And so, we ran. And so, of course, I won. Yes, I cheated, but it was worth it to see the look on her face as she streamed past the corner several seconds after me. I didn't fly, didn't need to. "Come on, Dreeg," I whispered into my head as I focused the screen and pulled silver lightning from his eyes, laser-zapping the mist from my leg. He grinned and puffed himself up, almost blowing me to the finish line. "Brilliant!" I shouted as I ran.

It was just too tempting. Anyway, what was the point in resisting now? I was too far in to go back.

"Don't mention it. It was a pleasure, my dear boy," he replied. "See? You can't resist me, can you? You can't resist what I can do for you. I can give you all this and more. And I ask so very little in return. Such a very little thing." His now-angelic-blue eyes smiled from a flawless face as we sat together on the mountain and looked down on the world. And still all I could see was the beauty of winning. I thought only of myself and pleasure. Of having it all.

I had let myself go, be carried along, sometimes believing that nothing else mattered and sometimes convincing myself that I had no choice.

"How the hell did you do that?" gasped Seraphina. "Was that what you meant before? About making things happen by thinking them?"

"Something like that. Let's train together next week," I said, changing the subject.

And that's what we did. Every day that week, the two of us spent our free time, break times, lunch breaks and evenings, running together and timing our performances. Discussed the best things to eat and when. Planned it like a war game. Recorded our times, gave each other incentives, spurred each other on in our different events.

I didn't forget about Tom. But the longer we didn't talk, the harder it was to work out what I could say. A couple of times, I caught his eye and almost went over to him, but each time, Dreeg steered me away and flooded my mouth with bitter notes. And it was always easier to walk away. My mobile phone was silent.

The heat grew. Everyone talked about it. "Never known a spell like it. When's it going to end?" "Just in time for the school holidays, I expect."

A week of focused calm. People stopped mentioning the newsletter. Roach asked two or maybe three times for the rest of my story and I used various standard delaying tactics, hoping he'd soon stop asking and then it would be the end of term. I worked, with Seraphina and Dreeg in their different ways, to strengthen my leg. Looking back, I suppose the "strengthen my leg" thing was a bit of a con. It wasn't really relevant that it was getting stronger. After all, I could just have won the race in one magic moment, without all this training stuff. It was more that Dreeg was strengthening my ability to use my power. All I cared about for the moment was winning at the interschools competition on Saturday and as far as I was concerned the training was all about making it look believable when it happened. I didn't look beyond that to what Dreeg might want me to do in return. If I had thought about it, I would perhaps have worried about what this "very little thing" was that he wanted me to do. But I wasn't looking that far ahead. I wasn't thinking about consequences.

And there's no doubt my control over my power did increase. Whether that was because he and I were working together, instead of fighting each other, I wasn't sure. Dreeg was certainly pleased with me. I could see it in his eyes. Not that pleasing him was anywhere at all in my mind. He was the way to achieve my selfish goal. Nothing else.

So all I really thought about during that week was running and winning. By Friday's athletics training my place in the team was assured and my confidence was strong. Reluctantly, Mum and even Dad had to agree that there was no reason for me not to run. When I thought of it, melting banana toffee came to my lips and a yellow butterfly sang around my head.

Laura went out that Friday night.

Dad didn't want her to go. "That man hasn't been

caught." He meant the man in the news, the one who'd attacked a girl.

"That was miles away," said Mum. "Anyway, it's all sorted out. Paul will look after her—she won't be on her own. You look great, Laur. Got enough money?" How could she think Laura looked great? Didn't she see what I saw?

Laura was dressed as skimpily as ever. Her skin wet as canal water in the dark. A spider sat on each big eye and dripped blood onto her sucking lips. She did not look at me as she whispered, "Good night, baby brother. Oh, and your little running race. Sorry I can't make it. Break a leg, won't you? For me."

Paul knocked on the door to collect her. So polite to Mum and Dad, it made my flesh crawl. I smelt a Nativity play. His face a mask. His eyes empty. "Cripple," he snided at me as he passed, his large-knuckled hand on Laura's body as he let her go first through the door.

"Later," whispered Dreeg. "He'll wait. They'll both wait."

"But not for long," slithered the masked metal man, breathing excitement in the shadows. "Not for long at all. I hope you are good and ready, dirty little tart. I have watched you long enough, I have. Oh, I have, I have. Waited long enough, I have."

I put Laura and Paul away. Focus on the race, Luke.

That night, as I lay waiting for sleep beneath a thin sheet, my thoughts were on nothing but the next day. I had every reason to believe that I would win.

My sleep at first was deep and healing but toward the end of the night I had a dream that felt nothing at all like a dream. It was as vivid as real.

The Dream

I was high on a mountain, scrambling over rocks, following Dreeg toward the summit. Above the clouds we walked, in air thin as gauze, dizzy as lemonade. I carried a tray of fruit, which I was taking as a present to the king on the mountain, because I owed him a favor. One of the fruits was poisoned and I knew which one it was. I wanted him to choose that one but it was pulsing with purple smoke, giving the game away. If he knew I was trying to poison him he would not take it but would throw me down the mountain, where I would crush my head on the rocks and my leg would dissolve into a million flecks of fog.

If I poisoned him I would be on my own. Which I did not want. And yet I did. Didn't and did. I understood precisely what I meant.

We came to the door in the cave at the top of the mountain. Dreeg, with a paper crown on his head, turned to me and pointed down through the clouds with a huge syringe full of bubbles in his hand. I could see everything below, the world on a plate. Enormous.

"I want it all," he said. "The king has promised it to me if I can prove my power and I want it. I want to be king." And his hair started to glow, until it burst into flames and was a burning tree around his head as he laughed a manic laugh. "And you. You can be king with me. Wouldn't you like that? You and I? King together? You could have everything you want. If you just help me. You and I, Luke. Ruling the world."

I offered him the tray of fruit and his spindly fingers hovered over each piece as he dribbled over them. Hovered over the feathery peach, hesitated over the neon strawberries, touched the poisoned purple heart-shaped nectarine.

"Don't!" a shout came from somewhere. "Not that one! It's poisoned!" I saw his shock. His eyes blazing ochre angry.

He was Seraphina suddenly. She was taking the smoking fruit and smiling as she licked its skin. Dreeg was watching her with a grin. I threw the tray down and knocked the fruit from her hand. Too late. Her tongue was turning blue. But she wasn't Seraphina after all. She was Laura. The fruit burst and lilac nail varnish dripped from it, burning a hole in everything it touched.

It burnt through her mouth, sieving through the flesh of her throat and sliding onto the ground below. I saw the horror in her eyes as she realized what I had done. She fizzed and twisted into liquid, burning lava making holes in the ground, turning it into pumice. Crumbling beneath our feet, the earth gave way and I fell through the mountain, clutching the ground, desperately trying to hold something solid.

Tumbling, twisting, I screamed as I fell. Then I was riding on Amber's back and we were flying. I saw Dreeg's face inches from mine and he was furious. "You stupid boy! What have you done? I needed you! The world was mine for the asking but I needed you. I needed your soul and you promised it to me for winning the race for you."

"I won the race!" I shouted as we landed on a spider's-web net. I tried to stand on the bouncing surface, struggling to keep my balance with the help of a giant wooden spoon as Amber growled at Dreeg. "I won the race! Not you, jellied urine. Not you, rotten liver. I did it without you."

His empty eyeless face sneered. "No, you can't do anything without me. Haven't you noticed? Don't you remember? The point is, I am you. Haven't you got it yet? I am you."

A flash of lightning. An orchestra in my head. I stood completely still. "Ahhh! I am you? You are me? Is that right, Dreeg? If you are me and I am you, then what are you without me? What can you *do* without me? You can't do anything, can you? You are like mistletoe. You are a parasite. A flea. My dad squashes fleas between his fingers and they pop when they die. A tiny pop. And then he puts them on the fire. Or in the bin. It really doesn't matter when they're squashed."

He shriveled, hissing into his own acid. I smelt sulfur. He picked up a pair of crutches and hit me over the head with them. I exploded into stars and we ran, Laura, Seraphina,

116

Amber and I. Tom was there, shouting at me to keep going. Mr. Breslin fired a gun into the air. Dad was directing the fire engines through the burning woods as we ran, chased by flames. The thick grass tangled our feet and we kept running past the same tree, over and over and over again, the same tree, never getting nearer the hut. And each time more of the tree was burning, until it seemed it must collapse in a puff of ash.

"Don't turn round!" shouted Seraphina. But I did, and I saw Amber running into the flames and I screamed but could not run toward them myself because I had another purpose, but I did not know what it was. No matter how hard I tried, I could not think what it was I was trying to do. A huge bubble of water was trapped in my lungs and I wanted to stop it all, stop everything and only cry.

The path forked silently and I went one way. I was on my own again. Looking at a hut in a clearing. A fairy-tale hut with sparkling windows and smoke blowing candy floss from the gingerbread chimney. An ax in a log. A scream came from the hut and a man came out, looking around to see if anyone had heard. I froze behind a tree with purple seeping fruit. The man was thin and cruel, with a dirty coat and grinning hands and a yellow face and the smell of petrol on his breath. As he looked toward the tree where I was, I saw his eyes, his one blue one and one completely white. He turned back to go inside the hut and Laura's scream swelled out when the door opened.

Her scream stopped suddenly and I ran to the door of the hut and banged and banged and banged until the metal man came out, who was, and wasn't, couldn't have been and yet had to be, the old man with the coat. His mask was stretched as though he was trying to smile from beneath it.

"Yes?" he asked, politely, looking at the ax. In one hand he held a syringe and in the other a giant lipstick.

I looked past him into the hut and saw a hand with lilac fingernails, dripping blood and hanging limp. "Yes?" he asked again.

I woke with tears flooding down my face. The tears continued to pour down, even when I realized that I had been dreaming. As I tried to sort out what was real and what was not, I was left with the absolute knowledge that something had happened to Laura.

And I was right. She had not come back.

The Apocalypse Begins

As soon as I realized this, I knew something else, too. That it mattered. That it really mattered to me. The dream had changed everything. An electric shock jolting me back to what was real and important and worth knowing. Real brother-and-sister stuff.

I could see that her room had not been slept in. Her tiny clothes were unconscious on the floor and wherever they had been left by my stupid anger the night before. Dirty cotton-wool balls cluttered the dressing table and you could have written a message in the dust. I wished I could write a message to say I was sorry.

I rushed into Mum and Dad's room. "Laura's not home! Her bed's not been slept in. Something's happened. The man. On the news. Dad!"

They sat up in shock, then realized what I was saying.

"For goodness' sake, Luke! She phoned late last night— she's at Jessica's house. She's not meant to be back. Go back to bed."

"But I had a nightmare. I—"

"Just a nightmare, Luke. Don't you think Jessica's parents would have phoned if something had happened? Go away. Go back to bed or go and get some breakfast or something. We're lying in." And they pulled the duvet over their heads.

But I knew that Laura was not all right.

I dressed quickly and went downstairs. I didn't know what I was going to do. Mum and Dad didn't believe anything was wrong so it was up to me. I fed Amber and ate a peanut butter sandwich. It was 7:30 A.M.

I wanted Tom, needed him. But it was too early to phone his house. His mum would only ask questions. He would have come without questioning. I knew that now, now that it was too late. All I could do was leave a message on his mobile and hope he woke up soon and turned it on.

"meet me in wds. pls. urgnt. sorry."

I left a note on the kitchen table saying I'd gone for a jog and closed the back door quietly.

Dreeg sat in a corner of my brain, waiting to see what I would do. Whether it was worth rousing himself. He smelt like a rat fattened in a sewage pipe. He could wait. I understood his evil perfectly now, but I could not let him know me.

Early yellow Saturday colors. The taste of melting tree juice. The heat of recent weeks had seeped into the land, the trees, the houses, so that even this early in the morning the warmth pulsed like bees. Still and silent, with no breeze to breathe, the air began to swell. A tiny fog of a headache stroked the back of my eyes. I squinted into the glare.

I set off toward the woods.

Seraphina was waiting there. No space in my head to wonder how she knew.

"Something's happened to Laura," I said.

"That's what it was," she said. "I knew there was something. I'd been dreaming of fire. When I woke up I felt totally weird, tangled wool. And really scared of something." She looked at me nervously. "I could taste fruit, but rotten, kind of blue acid."

Just then I noticed her fingernails. Lilac. She saw me looking. She laughed with slight embarrassment. "My lucky color. For this afternoon." The athletics competition. Two o'clock. But first we had to do something. I wished she wasn't wearing lilac nail varnish. The metal man sniggered and played slowly with a rope in his hands.

Dreeg whispered in my ear. "Hurry, Luke. You want to be in on this, don't you? To see it all happen? This is the end of your story now. The final test of your power. The woods. She's in the woods."

"She's somewhere in the woods," I said. "Come on." And we began to run together, side by side. Our breathing even and the smell of honey in my mouth. I focused on the gold in my leg and sprang on steel muscles. No trace of fog, as Dreeg urged me on. Power.

I looked at my phone. Nothing from Tom.

We came to a place where two wide paths stretched into the haze. And two narrow ones into the darkness between the trees. Which one to take?

"Well?" asked Dreeg.

"Well what?"

"Well, how are you going to find her?"

"I'm going to smell her fear."

"Fantastic! What does her fear smell like, Luke?" he hissed.

I looked inside, focused, controlled. Her fear smelt ripe, leaking. Leaves blowing along a pavement at Halloween. A vase tumbling slowly to the ground. An evil nurse breathing fast as she tampers with the child's tubes. I saw a girl sitting in a hut, tied, gagged, wet with sweat. A masked man watching her, plucking petals from black tulips and chanting aloud and slowly, "She wants it, she wants it not, she wants it, she wants it not—"

"Quick!" I urged, and we ran along one wide path toward the fear. Staying close to the trees, we moved at a rhythmic pace. Steady, controlled, strong.

With every minute the sun burnt more fiercely. Gravy heat, unbreathable. Sweat leaking. Blood pulsing. Eyes swimming red. Brain swelling in my skull.

Suddenly I could smell smoke, real smoke and a fresh burnt-match smell. I stopped. Seraphina could smell it, too. We looked down. The grass at our feet was on fire. Tiny flames, innocent-seeming but growing, fanned by a breeze from nowhere. I stamped on them. Each time I stamped one out, another bled onto the grass until they were springing up like Triffids. Frantically we stamped and stamped until eventually no more appeared and the breeze died into nothing again. Smoke bubbled menacingly from the ground.

"You'll need to do better than that, my boy," said Dreeg. "What will you do when the fire really starts? Eh? A bit of stamping is not going to have any effect at all when it really gets going."

122

But I hardly heard him because I could hear something else. Whimpering, crying. A pale green smell. And shuffling sounds in the bracken. I signaled Seraphina to keep dead quiet. I pointed in the direction the noise was coming from and led her quickly but quietly into the trees a short way away. We watched and waited as the sound came nearer.

Revelation

A boy stumbled out of the undergrowth and collapsed on the ground. His tracksuit was filthy, his hair plastered greasy. Brown streaks washed down his face, and his arms were bleeding from scratches. His tracksuit trousers were wet with urine. It was Paul. An ugly inside part of me smiled but most of all I thought of Laura and fear took over.

We rushed toward him and he stumbled to his feet in panic, trying to run away. He was easy to catch and my rugby tackle brought my face close to his stink. He started to scream but I covered his dribbling with my hand and whispered in his ear, "Shut up, Paul, you ugly little creep. It's Luke. Where's Laura? Where the bloody hell's Laura? What have you done with her?"

Paul began to cry, huge desperate snorting sobs. Ugly to watch. "Hit him!" urged Dreeg, wobbling with pleasure at Paul's suffering. I don't hit people but I did then, and with more enjoyment than I should. Just to cure his hysteria. Not to injure him. A slap on the face, but it worked. He stopped his noise and stared at me, shocked.

"Where's Laura?" I repeated.

"A man . . . I don't know . . . I woke up and she was gone and—"

"Is that all?" asked Seraphina.

"Answer her, creep," I snarled when Paul didn't reply. But he could not take his eyes off my face, as if struggling to remind himself of who he was and what he had done.

"What?" he asked blankly, still not seeming to notice that Seraphina was there.

"Is that all?" I said. "What do you mean by a man? What man?"

"I didn't see anyone. I just thought. It had to be a man. The man in the news. Isn't that what you think?" and he started blubbering again.

"What were you doing in the woods, anyway? Laura was meant to be staying with Jessica."

"That was the story. My dad thought I was staying at Tad's. Everyone thought we were all staying at someone's house but a load of us came to sleep in the woods. Only the others went home—said the ground was too hard. Laura and I stayed. And then when I woke up, about two hours ago, she'd gone. No," he said, looking down. "Not what you think. Separate sleeping bags. She's not like that, whatever you think. That stuff, in the toilets, it was—" and he mumbled something.

I shook him. "It was what? It was bloody what?"

"A lie." His nose was dribbling.

The swelling of relief was strangled by the horror of what I had done and thought.

Paul was speaking faster now, looking at me anxiously as though I must forgive him. "I wanted to get help, honest. If I'd known which way, I'd have gone after them."

"Yeah, well, you didn't, did you? You're just a useless creep who can't even look after his own girlfriend. Are you coming with us now?"

"There's no way he's coming with us," said Seraphina scathingly. "He'll get in the way and he can't run fast enough. Look at him. God, he's pathetic."

"What are you going to do? I wouldn't be any good," said Paul to me, terrified. Dreeg was shaking his head.

"Baggage, Luke. Excess baggage. Lose him. You wanted him to pay, didn't you? Now's your chance. Waste him."

I could have done anything—after all, I had the power, didn't I?—but he was just a blubbering baby and, best of all, he knew I knew just what he was. I pulled up the screen and wrapped him in a cocoon like a spider's egg parcel. I pulled a sleepy mist over his eyes and left him, lying safely under a tree, sleeping like a baby with his thumb in his mouth. Seraphina laughed. "Rock-a-bye, baby," she sang, and butterflies melted out of her mouth and fell dead to the ground.

Dreeg growled. "What was the point of that, Luke? You could have killed him, cut his legs off, turned his skin green and sliced the flesh off his bones with a razor blade. Why didn't you do that?"

"No need. Why would I do that?"

"Because you can. Because he deserves it. And because you hate him."

"Not really. Not anymore."

"You disappoint me sometimes, Luke. You could do so much more. I know you want the same as me. To win. At any cost."

"Yes, well, let's get a move on, shall we? Are you helping me or not?" If he knew what I was planning, he would fight. I had to string him along for now.

"Yes, of course, Luke, of course I'm helping you. I'm having the hugest amount of fun helping you. It's becoming extremely thrilling, I can tell you. Watching how the story you started is going to end. Watching you use your power. With my help, let's not forget. Always with my help." He burped wetly, yellow froth bubbling from his throat. While I needed him with me, in me, I wished I needn't look at him.

We left Paul safely hidden in the undergrowth and I fixed the place in my head in case we needed to come and fetch him later. "I'm thirsty, Luke," said Seraphina. She looked exhausted. "I didn't bring anything, did you?"

Neither of us had brought anything to drink or eat. As the heat increased and our sweat soaked into our clothes, the need for water was frightening.

"There's a stream through here somewhere," I lied. "Moon water, soft as a butterfly's breath, tastes like crystal. Follow me," and I led her through some trees until very soon we could hear the sound of glass beads and saw the tiny trickle running between clean stones. So clear was it, that we were not seeing the water itself, only the light skittering from it and the pebbles below. We drank as much as we could, leaning forward with our heads turned sideways, to catch the water as it bubbled and swelled.

"Beautiful, Luke!" snarled Dreeg. "Look what you can do! Look what I've taught you! Beautiful power." A fat tongue flickered from his mouth, licking up the spittle.

We soaked our clothes in water to keep us cool for a while longer. Back on the path we began to jog again, trying to keep to the edge, in the shade. The smell of fear grew stronger. It was turning red at the edges, the orange-red of fire.

We ran on, our breath coming in shorter gasps, the strength seeping from our legs.

I heard a rumble in the distance. I stopped, gesturing to Seraphina, and we slipped into the darkness of the trees. It faded away. A horse? Or faraway thunder? The weight of the day's heat compressed my head and a trickle of sweat dripped down my back.

Seraphina looked at me. "I need to rest," she said. "Five minutes. I'm sorry."

"Of course," I said, but I wished she didn't need to. I looked at her. The softness of her made my heart lurch. The musical notes around her hair were tiny, delicate as cells.

"Weak," said Dreeg. "She's weak. You've got to get a move on. You've got to find out what's happened to Laura. Don't you want to know?"

I snapped. "Know? I don't want to *know*. I want to rescue her, you moron." I couldn't help it. Besides, we were so nearly there. The rat-gray smell of her fear was all around me now.

"Oh, surely not? Surely not? What a pathetically drippy end to a beautifully terrifying story! What will Roach think about it? Surely you can't be planning a happy ending, can you? Please tell me you're not. What about her punishment? Doesn't she deserve an unhappy ending?"

"This isn't about my story. This is about the fact that Laura's in danger."

"So? She deserves it. And it's what you wanted. You did all this. You set it up. With my help, of course. As usual."

"No, I didn't. You did it, in the part of me that is you."

"Are you sure? It was what you wanted. You wanted it enough for it to happen. You willed it. You caused it."

"No, it was a thought. That's all. It came into my head— part of my anger. It doesn't mean I wanted it. I rejected it."

"Really? Look inside yourself, Luke."

Inside myself I could hear the metal man breathing and Laura trying to scream behind a sticky gag. And the shame like a jackal, shaking me. I couldn't have done this. Yet I knew I had. However much I wanted to blame the parasite, I had welcomed it in. And now I would have to make everything right. Myself.

"Come on, Seraphina. We have to go. This way." I set off into the woods, off the main path and through the trees. We stumbled through bracken with wet, rotten roots, sank our feet into oily eons of leaf mold, pushed aside fingered branches with nails that tried to scratch our eyes out. As we moved further and further from the path, the darkness thickened. The trees were so matted, so ancient, that little light could penetrate. Creatures scuttled blindly away from the noises of the first humans they had ever heard.

Suddenly one leg dropped into nothing and I fell, landing facedown in yellow fungus. I felt a ripping sound in my ankle. Pain like a hundred bee-stings shot up my leg. I lay, holding my breath against the agony. Wanting to give up, wishing someone could just take over. What could I hope to achieve, anyway? What a stupid, over-the-top, totally unlikely kids' adventure story. Real people just didn't run around woods rescuing their sisters from goodness knows what. Yet the pain was real. Breath-stealingly real. Fire-hot.

"Deal with it, Luke," sneered Dreeg. "It's all to test you, hone your power. You can do anything, remember. If you choose."

No choice. Wearily, focused on the screen. Picked a clean syringe from the shelf. Drew back the plunger. Pushed it into my leg. Imagined the empty white lack of pain and stood up, wiping the sweat and slime from my eyes as best I could. So . . . damned . . . easy.

Dreeg smiled. "Isn't it wonderful to be able to do things like that, Luke? That's what you get for staying with me, being part of me."

"Are you all right?" asked Seraphina, her breath in my ear. A lick of cinnamon. A fairground, ice-cream-van-innocent tune.

"Yeah, sorry. You OK to go on?" And we carried on, into the darkness of the woods. I had lost all sense of direction. I knew only that Laura was in here. Somewhere. I shivered. It was cold inside this cave of trees.

On we went as fast as we could. Our breath rasped now. How much longer could we run?

Suddenly Seraphina screamed and leapt back, pointing at the ground in front of us. At first I couldn't see what she was looking at but then I made out the huge shape of a spider, staring at us, two brown legs in the air. I'm not frightened of spiders. I stepped toward it. It slithered away into the bracken. And sat there.

Seraphina screamed again and started lashing at her own head. I saw that another spider, as large as the first, was in her hair, burrowing its way in. I swiped at it. It stuck to my hand. Quivering. I tried frantically to shake it off but it started exuding sticky strands and wrapping them around my knuckles with a hissing noise. Another spider landed on my shoulder. I could see two more coming toward me. These were not normal spiders. These had eyes and brains. These were planning.

"Come on, Luke," jeered Dreeg. "You're losing this one. And you'll get no help from the girl, you know. Weak, she is, and no good with spiders. You can't rely on her."

The spider on my shoulder had started weaving itself around my neck. Its legs ran over my mouth, leaving the taste of petrol. I spat, but the taste was seeping inside. I must not swallow. I tightened my lips. A sting pierced my ankle and I kicked out. A spider flew from my shoe and lay nearby, breathing, waiting. My ankle started to throb and swell. I knew—with cold horror—that I had been bitten.

I wanted to scream but I couldn't breathe. The spider from my shoulder stopped on the back of my neck. It stung and I felt the creeping liquid of its poison slip into my veins. Within seconds the world started to go black and chilled. I heard myself distantly calling Seraphina's name. Fading. To nothing.

Poison

The **nothing** grew louder.

I was aware of a crashing noise. Repeated thumps. Felt pain smash into my shoulder, back, leg, arm. Hard enough to bring me awake. I was on my hands and knees. Seraphina was standing in front of me with a huge stick. Dead spiders lay around.

"Sorry," she said, shaking. "I couldn't touch them. I had to use a stick. Hope I didn't hurt you too much."

"You killed the spiders," I mumbled, spitting and retching. "That's all I care 'bout." My voice started to disappear into the distance again. "Bitten. Don't . . . good. Help." Struggle to find air. Lungs shrinking. Fear.

"Sit down," and I felt her touch me. "Let's have a look. Where?"

"Ankle . . . neck." They throbbed and burnt. When she rolled my sock back, I could see that my ankle was red and swollen, with a tiny black mark in the middle. And the black was spreading. Blood poisoning. The swelling on my neck was spreading to my throat. I was going to die. My eyes dissolved and I could not keep them open. Oddly, from a cloud, floating, I began to think it didn't matter, that maybe this was how I had to pay. It didn't feel so bad, if this was dying. Not so hard to do. Just like falling asleep. Spinning on cotton wool. Not minding.

Dreeg was looking worried. "Luke, wake up," he said urgently, rattling my brain. I couldn't. I couldn't remember how to wake up. So much easier just to be asleep. I couldn't remember anything about what I was meant to be doing. Why was I here? Who was I? Did anything really matter? What was awake, anyway?

"Luke! Luke! Wake up. You can do it." Dreeg was now neon with fear. He needed me, of course. I smiled drunkenly.

"What? Do?" whispered in my head.

"Save yourself," he urged.

"Why for?"

"For me."

"Sod you." Smilingly.

"Oh, for Laura, then, for Seraphina, for running, anything you damn well want. Just stay with me."

Seraphina's voice came through the mist, shouting, yelling. "Luke, for God's sake, stay awake, please." Iced coffee on my lips as she bent her face toward mine where I lay on the forest floor. Then other noises, shouts, rustlings, wetness.

Someone was shaking me and seemed to be licking my face. And through the cold haze, I heard Grandpa's voice. "Everything works out for the best in the best of all possible worlds, Luke," he was saying. "But if you're not in it, you can't win it." He threw a rope, which curled and swizzled, slicing through the space between us. With a huge effort, though I didn't know why I was bothering, I grabbed it, swam to the surface and forced the screen into focus. Dreamt sunlight, drank magic, filtered my blood, sucked the poison out and spat it onto the ground.

I was surrounded. I didn't know how this could have happened but I was surrounded by Seraphina, Tom and Amber.

"How—?"

"We heard you screaming, thrashing about in the bushes," said Tom, grinning properly at me for the first time in days. "Not difficult."

"But we're miles from the path," I said.

"You're not, actually. Not more than fifty meters."

"How did you know which path? Amber?" Tom nodded. We both knew there was no need for any sorries. I put my arms round Amber, who licked my face as though it was a huge game. I hugged her tightly, breathing in the biscuit smell of her and hiding my feelings in her fur. I wished she wasn't here. It was dangerous and she would not be good at being quiet. This was not some Famous Five adventure where Timmy the dog saves the day and frightens the baddies into submission. She wasn't that kind of dog and this wasn't the sort of story that has such an easy ending.

"I got your message. What's it all about, anyway? What are you doing?" asked Tom. I told him about Laura, how no one believed me that something had happened to her.

"But your mum says she's at Jessica's house," said Tom. "She saw me as I was going down the road and she ran after me. She's mad with you because she said if you were going for a run, why didn't you take Amber? She said she doesn't have time to take her for a walk. Anyway, as you can see, I said I'd take her. Good job I did. You look terrible. And what's all that stuff on your face and neck?'"

"I just fell in something. Listen, Tom. This is serious. Don't ask how I know. There's just weird stuff been happening and I'm pretty sure there's a man who's got Laura."

"Not the man on the news? You're joking."

I didn't know if that was what had happened but it was bad enough without the rest of it.

"Well, we'd better get help," Tom said. "We can't do anything on our own."

"No, there's no time. I know where she is."

He started to say something.

"Don't ask. I just know. Come on. We need to get back to the path." I didn't want to come across the spiders again, didn't want to think about them. I had changed my mind about not being frightened of spiders and I vowed that I would never again put one in Laura's schoolbag. Now I understood what cruelty was. And what I was.

With Tom leading the way, soon we were back on the path, with a crossroads in front of us. Three ways we could go. I knew all these paths, but I had never seen the hut I was looking for. I closed my eyes, inhaled her fear like a bloodhound.

A girl sits blindfolded in a hut, her lilac nails cutting deep into the palms of her hands. In the shadows is a man, squatting on the floor like a beast. He strikes matches one by one and lets them burn until his fingers melt. Three dead rabbits hang from a hook in the ceiling. The man stops burning his matches and drops them to the floor. One is still alight but he doesn't notice. It scorches the floor, smoking. As he walks toward the window, a breeze fans unnoticed and a tiny lick of flame slides over the dry-as-bones boards.

Another fire is growing in the forest, sauntering toward the hut, grazing everything it finds.

A knife sits on the table. Its blade glints. It is sharp enough to slice through flesh in one soft butter movement.

The man picks a spider from the window ledge and puts it on the girl's leg and watches it crawl toward her thigh. She does not know what it is but she screams. He does not mind if she screams. No one can hear her here in the middle of the woods.

He takes the knife and softly runs the blade across his thumb.

"Stop!" I shouted aloud. Tom looked at me.

"This way. Run!" And the running began again. Along the dried-up path. Through the everywhere heat. The silence broken by the pounding of our feet and the blood in our ears. And our breath rasping over stick-dry tongues. Then to the left where a tiny pathway forced its way between the trees. We slowed to a halt. The grasses were flattened. I pointed to some broken branches at shoulder height. I touched them. Freshly broken. I led the way and we followed the darkening path as quietly and quickly as we could.

There was no breeze but something carried the smell of smoke toward us. We looked at each other and knew what we were each thinking. But we had no choice. We had to go on to where Laura was. Something black lay on the ground.

I stopped. It was a petal, a tulip petal. I don't know much about flowers but I did know one thing: there are no black tulips anywhere in the world. We carried on, following the trail of black tulip petals.

We all saw it at the same moment. A stick, stuck in the ground. On the path right in front of us. For us. Blocking the way. And on the top of it, pierced through its body, a bird. Black. Bright eyes open. Watching. Seraphina put her hand over her mouth. Tom looked at me.

Destruction

"**W**e keep going," I said. "It's nothing, just some kids. Keep going and don't look back."

I pushed them in front of me as we passed it. I did look back. It was still watching. Its head had turned full circle. Shutting my mind to the horror, I erased its eyes closed with my thoughts and turned to follow the others.

And then, at last, we saw the hut. Although I'd never been to this particular one before, I knew that it was an old forestry commission hut. They used to use them for storing tools, the fire brushes, tools for cutting back vegetation, things like that. They don't use them anymore—instead you'll get someone like my dad driving around in a jeep and shouting orders for tools on his mobile phone.

This hut was in a clearing, about fifty meters away from any trees. Outside it was an ax, resting with its blade buried deep in the flesh of a tree stump. A large rainwater tank rusted nearby.

I could smell something like frightened cats.

On the far side of the clearing, smoke was coming from the trees. No flames could be seen yet but we could hear the crackling as it came. Amber began to growl and Seraphina soothed her, holding her lead tightly. We stayed hidden by the trees, thinking. What now?

We needed help. I took out my mobile. No signal. I looked at Tom. He looked at his phone. No signal. Odd.

In the distance a fire engine. Here and now, nothing but throbbing fear. The heat a lead blanket, smothering. My brain was hurting. Think. For God's sake, think of something.

"Come on, Luke, think of something," said Dreeg from the depths of my head. His fingers writhed like marshworms. "Show us all what you can do."

I didn't know where the man was. He could be in the shed. Or he might be somewhere in the trees. He could be watching us. Or he could be harming Laura. At this very moment.

"Wait here," I said to the others, and I moved around the clearing a little way, toward the smoke, to face the side of the hut without a window. Without breathing, I ran the short distance to the hut and flattened myself against the side wall. My brain ached with the effort of keeping my leg strong and my heart quiet. I could hear nothing inside. Slowly, avoiding sticks, I edged my way round to the back and moved closer to the window. Thick with ancient dirt. I peered in. Gradually I could make out some shapes. A table. On the table a knife. Things hanging from the ceiling. And Laura, definitely Laura, tied to a chair, with her head slumped forward, still. Very still and very silent.

Then another figure in the hut, manlike, stood up. Suddenly the hut was filled with light. The door had opened and the man was going out. I flattened myself again and darted my head from left to right. If the man was coming round the hut, I didn't know which way he would come.

"Come on, Luke, get a grip, you silly boy. The story's running away with you. Laura could be dead already and you haven't controlled it at all. Do you want some ideas?"

"Get lost, scum. I'm doing this myself. I don't need you." Dreeg shriveled and spat at me.

"You can't do it," he snarled. "You do need me. Remember what I told you? You can't do it without me."

"Watch me," I whispered. "Just watch me, weakling." Dreeg seethed and scratched the back of my eyes until they watered. Lime-green razors. I dug a hole in the slime of my head and forced his fatness in, squelching inch by inch, spat glue in his blank eyes and sealed the hole with a lead lid.

I saw the man go toward the woods, toward the smoke. Turn once to look at the hut. He didn't see me but I saw his eyes, one blue, one white. In his hands a rope and matches. Not the metal man. A thin old man with a dirty coat and big greedy grinning hands. A yellow face and the smell of petrol on his breath. Eerie eyes, one blue and one rheumy white. I had seen him in my dream. I had heard about him on the news.

He went into the trees near where the smoke was and as soon as I was sure he had gone, I ran back to Tom and Seraphina. Told them to keep a lookout, one on each side of the clearing. They were to whistle if the man came back. I ran back to the hut and pushed open the door. It wasn't locked. Inside, the smell was foul. I held my sleeve against my mouth. Coming inside from the brightness outside, it was difficult to see anything. I could just make out Laura's shape and I moved toward her. Something brushed against my head. Something soft and wet. I touched it. Rabbit. Dead and wet warm.

Laura was cold and still. I shook her. "Laura, wake up!" She didn't respond. I felt the gag on her mouth. Tight, sticky-tape. I began to pull it off. The pain of it roused her and she struggled. "Laura, it's me, Luke. Stay still while I get this stuff off. The man's gone. Shhh, it's Luke." And she started to cry. I felt the sadness ooze up inside me, too, but by clenching my mouth and holding my breath I could push it back.

Thunder. Distant fire engines. Then louder thunder. And a scream but no whistles. What was happening? Where were Tom and Seraphina? I ripped the tape off Laura's mouth, caring how much it hurt but knowing I had to do it. Grabbed the knife from the table and sawed through the ropes around her wrists and feet. A shadow. Framed in the doorway so that I could not see him properly was the masked man, holding Seraphina by the rope around her throat. Out of his mouth he pulled a lipstick, which he used to paint her lips messy poisonous red.

"Look what I found," he said. "Another filthy, dirty girl." I looked inside my head and saw that Dreeg had begun to squeeze out of his prison, oozing and smiling as he re-formed.

"Back again, Luke. You can't get rid of me that easily. I want to watch and I will."

As the man came into the hut, pushing Seraphina in front of him, I heard a helicopter clatter overhead. Instinctively I looked up.

"It's for the fires," said the man, gesturing with his head at the helicopter noise. "They're spreading. As fast as anyone can put them out, they're spreading. A natural cleanser, fire. Clears out all the weaklings, the weeds, the poison, the rubbish, the filth. Lets Nature start all over again. Nature, that's the thing. Nature clean and pure. Not like a dirty, filthy slut." His hands twisted the rope round Seraphina's throat.

I still had the knife in my hand. I held it up, to let him see. "Let her go," I said. "Just let her go and I'll say nothing about it," I lied. But he just tightened the rope more and her frightened eyes swelled, her lips turning gray. She started to droop.

"Wrong way round, little boy," said the man. "You drop the knife. Now." He lifted his arm slowly and Seraphina hung from his hand. His strength seemed enormous. I dropped the knife. He pushed Seraphina to the floor and tied her to the table legs. She struggled, gasping for breath. Laura still slumped on her chair, with her head forward, as though unaware of anything. I tried to see if she was breathing, but I couldn't tell. I couldn't move but my mind sprinted.

The man walked over to Laura and, as he passed so close that I could smell his breath, I saw that he was not the masked man anymore but the eerie-eyed man with the filthy coat. His body moved with an ease that had not been there before. He pulled a match from somewhere and lit it. He held it a breath away from Laura's hair.

"Now," said the man, looking at me from the shadows. "You. Walk. Out. Leave her."

Dreeg smiled and rubbed his hands together. "Beautiful, Luke! You're going to burn her! Fire makes such a brilliant ending. The apocalypse, as she burns for her badness! Brilliant imagination! We'll go so far together!" His scarlet face shone in the excitement and I knew exactly what I had to do.

I walked, as I was told. Thinking, I know what I'm doing. I've got a plan. I walked out of the hut, followed by the man. I could smell his ancient grease. I heard the door close. In front of me part of the forest was now on fire, trees crackling and things screaming. The wall of flames was leaping higher. "Don't look round," said an empty voice, "or I burn the slag. Walk toward the fire. And don't stop, because I will be watching. And if you walk all the way to the fire, and into the fire, like a good boy, I will let the little slut go. Fly free, like a little bird." I knew he was lying but I pretended not to. And who was he talking about? Laura or Seraphina?

Out of the corner of my eye, I saw Tom. I only saw him because I knew where to look. He was well hidden in the trees. Carefully, with my hand in front of my body so that the man behind me could not see, and painting the inside of my brain white so that Dreeg could not read it, I gestured to Tom, hoping that he would trust me, trying to tell him that he should stay there and wait.

As I walked, with the rasping breath behind me, Dreeg was grinning in excitement. "This is wonderful, Luke. What are you planning? This is so dramatic, you walking toward the woods, pretending you have no choice, while the hut burns down with Laura in it." As he said that, I heard breaking glass and without looking round knew the hut was beginning to burn. I could hear screaming and the man laughed. "Nature's way," he said.

No time to lose. It had to be now.

"Now, Dreeg! I want to fly!"

"Fly, then, if that's what you want. But I'm surprised you're leaving Seraphina in the hut, too. Still, I knew you'd tire of her. Weak, she was, just like them all. No better, and no help to you. They can burn together in your fire. Your fire, my boy, all yours."

I blocked him out as I ran toward the burning trees, and flew on a frozen arc of lemon sherbet. Smooth as pearl was the air I drank. Purest white piccolo notes were the sounds I saw. I could have flown forever, away toward the light, with Dreeg laughing in my head, but I made myself look down. I could see Tom running across the clearing toward the smoking hut with Amber. Saw them reach the door and open it. Saw the man turn and see them. Saw him race back toward the hut. Saw the flames in the forest, a growing wall of fire eating up the trees around the little clearing. Where all my friends were.

A crash of thunder, much closer than before. A darkening sky. And Dreeg, grotesque mass in my head, a tumor, a part of my brain that needed to be cut out forever and destroyed.

Flying was liquid heaven, but it was filth compared with losing my soul.

I turned to him and screamed. "You don't understand.

You never will. But I didn't, either, not before. Now, Dreeg, I want it to stop. *This* is my ending."

"Oh, not this again, silly boy. We've had this before, Luke. You know the score. Do we have to go over it again?" He smirked wearily, counting on his fingers. "You want to win, your silly little races, that running stuff. You want to be able to do this, this flying, this magic, this turning anything into anything. And as far as wanting to punish Laura is concerned, and even more wanting Seraphina, well, I gave you all that as well. I gave you all that you are. This power. And you took it, took it greedily, selfishly, willingly. You guzzled it. You stuffed it drooling into your greedy little mouth. And now it's all too late. You can't turn back time, you know. You've gone too far. Look at all you have done. All this destruction." He was insect-blood yellow in my brain. There was nothing human about him anymore, nothing to hang on to.

"But you forget, Dreeg. You need me, too. Remember on the mountain? My dream? When I discovered that you are *nothing* without me. Nothing but a little part of my brain. Well, I can get rid of you. You said if I flew with you and proved that I wanted it all to go, you to go, I could have that."

"Well, I lied."

"No, you didn't. You are lying now. I know you now because I know myself. Or the ugly part of myself that is you." From the screen in my head I selected a scalpel, fingering the blade unimaginably thin, thin and sharp as light, and I held it up, twisting it to show him how it gleamed cold. Inside my brain, I found the place where he was and I began to move the blade toward him. He squealed like a snail in the grasp of poison.

"No! Look, Luke! Look down there!" I didn't want to fall for that again. But I heard barking. Amber. I looked down and saw Amber run from the burning hut, her tail on fire, running straight toward the trees. The trees, which I could see would soon be engulfed by flames themselves. "Seraphina!" I screamed, and my scream flew like an arrow toward the hut, into her heart where she could hear me. "Get Amber!" And I saw her run from the hut, toward the burning trees, after my dog.

The Price

A **moment later,** the man came out of the hut and looked in the direction she had taken. He smiled as he locked the door and strode after her. "You've left your lovely tulips, dirty slag," he called. He ran into the fire with Seraphina.

"It's Seraphina, Luke—you never could resist when I offered you Seraphina," sneered Dreeg. "You can't save Seraphina if you throw it all away. To think I once thought you cared about her. Well, how was I to know? But I thought if I gave you so much, you'd be loyal to me, help me. It wasn't much to ask, was it? But now you've worked it out, haven't you?" While he spoke soothingly, he was edging slowly away from my reach. I knew that I would catch him. That this time he could not win.

"Yes, I've worked it out. It's simple. You needed me. You are like a parasite—you need a brain to work from. You chose mine. And you thought since you were in my brain that you knew me. You thought that if you gave me what you thought I wanted I'd be so bloody grateful I'd do anything for you. You are like the devil. You made me sell my soul. I should have refused and my sin is that I didn't. But I've changed my mind now. My soul is not for sale. I withdraw my offer. I make the rules. My life. My decisions. And I say you go. Completely. Destroyed."

"The girl," spat Dreeg. "What about Seraphina?"

"I don't believe you about Seraphina. She is more real than you know." Dreeg was edging away. Holes where his eyes should be, blank.

I lunged with the scalpel and started to dig him out of his hole, cutting him away. He began to squeal and writhe. "You can't! You can't! You'll regret it. Believe me, you'll regret it. And you're wrong about Seraphina after all. It's not that easy, not that tidy. You'll see. Just you waiiiiii—" And all of a sudden, my knife had cut the last dribble of him away and he was gone.

As I fell through the clawing, scraping branches of a tree, landing on the ground with a jarring crash, an immense pain cut across my eyes and through my head. I clutched my ears and rolled onto my knees on the scorched earth. I heard a scream. Seraphina or Laura, I couldn't tell. And a roar, rushing blood, thunder, all mixed up. In the deepest hole of my mind, the metal man melted into a squealing atom. A memory. I looked around me. Flames. I crawled to my feet, my leg thick with fog as I stumbled back toward the hut. Limping. No matter how I tried, I could not pour gold into my leg, could not make it strong. I was staggering over ground that steamed. How long would my shoes last? Was that the smell of burning rubber?

The door of the hut was still shut and I could hear noises inside. Smoke oozed from a broken window, too small to climb through. Three smashes with the ax, and the door flew open. Tom stumbled out, dragging Laura, both of them coughing and gagging. Ice spreading in my head. Wanting just to lie down and scream everything awake. I pulled off my T-shirt and soaked it with water from the tank. I wiped Laura's face and hair and scooped water in my hands for her to drink. Her eyes, screwed up against the smoke, streaked with dirt and tears, looked at mine and I heard her croak, "Sorry. So sorry." She was shaking and her skin was clammy cold despite the heat.

"Where's Amber and Seraphina?" I shouted at Tom. He couldn't speak without coughing. He only looked at me strangely and pointed toward the trees.

"You mean they haven't come back?" A glacier in my head.

But just then, before I had a chance to do anything, men burst into the clearing. Firemen. Six of them, shouting, "Over here! We've found them!" And within seconds we had oxygen masks on our faces and were being told not to talk. But I still didn't know where Seraphina and Amber were. Seraphina's name was a memory, fading fast.

I struggled to push aside the mask. "Did you find her? She went the same way you came from? And my dog? They were together. She went after my dog."

"Just relax, son. Don't talk. It'll be all right. We're taking the three of you home."

"But the girl?" I refused to give up. Though I could barely see through the pain in my head, I had to know.

"What girl?" She had disappeared. A candy-floss mist. Blown bubble.

"A girl. Long blond hair. And Amber. A retriever. Golden, too."

"They'll be OK, son. They'll be found."

I felt water on my face, cool drops of water. At the same time an enormous, shaking clap of thunder as the rains fell and the sky split into smithereens. The heat burst and evaporated as the water fell in huge rods around us. Spitting, the burnt ground sizzled. The fireman who held me smiled, shouted to the sky in relief. But I felt something crack inside and tears flood up from the deepest place inside me. Who was the girl who was missing? I couldn't remember her name. A shower of petals was falling on my face. I think I screamed as I passed out.

Sadness
Has a Blue Smell

The sirens again and the shaking. I know about ambulances now. The fear of dying. The not being able to move at all. Looking at ceilings and things being upside down.

"Your dog's fine," said the woman sitting next to me in the ambulance. "Tail a bit burnt but nothing that can't be fixed. The boy found her. Paul, is it? Found her wandering and took her home. Told the firemen about the three of you going into the woods."

I was glad Paul was all right. "Three? What about—?"

"Everyone's fine, Luke. Don't talk now, but everyone's fine. Your sister's in another ambulance. And Tom's here. Look." I looked to the side and saw Tom, lying with a mask on his face like me. His eyes smiled in relief at being alive.

"But—?" What was her name? Only her scent came to me, and that was faint as a whisper. Something like a warm cake. Sweet.

"That's enough. It's important not to talk. There's nothing

to worry about. Just rest your throat. And where's that phone? You can't use a mobile in an ambulance." My phone—the signal was back.

I didn't ask any more about the girl. I think I knew. I closed my eyes, but I wasn't sleeping. I didn't know if I would sleep again.

There was no pain in my head anymore. And when I hesitantly tried to focus the computer screen, nothing happened. I searched every corner of my brain, but I could find no sign of Dreeg. Not even the tiniest muon of his filth was there. Only the seashell sound of a harp. The taste of thyme. And the saddest blue smell in all the universe.

Cleansed

Of course, we missed the athletics competition. No question about that. Tom was coughing like an old man. My leg was fogbound. Mum and Dad were white with stress. And Laura couldn't talk. Gray as stone, she lay curled in her hospital bed in a room on her own, surrounded by people. The police wanted to talk to her, but the nurses wouldn't let them. Mum and Dad sat by her bed and stroked her hair as she lay there, absent. She had dug herself a hole inside her head and was not coming out.

I was allowed to go and see her. I limped into her room, dragging my leg. I loved the real heaviness of my limp. Mum moved aside to let me near the bed. "Can I speak to Laura?" I asked. "On my own?"

They left the room. Mum and Dad and I had already had the "What were you thinking of?" conversation. They couldn't be angry. After all, I was the one who had said something was wrong and they were eaten up with guilt at not believing me. Their main concern now was what had happened to Laura. And *that* I didn't know. I had to know.

I sat by her. Her face was cleaned, no tears, no smoke, no filth, no makeup. Her forehead was creased in a frown and her eyes were bolted shut. A transparent blue butterfly sat on her tangled hair and trembled. I touched her shoulder and she opened her eyes.

And when she saw me she cried. We cried together, our arms round each other. Afterward, I felt white-clean inside, so empty that I could have started my whole life all over again, afresh. That's what it was like. Being washed out inside.

"I was so frightened, Luke. You can't imagine. God, I was so scared. I thought I would die."

"What happened?"

She told me everything. She'd got out of her sleeping bag and walked into the trees where they'd left a bag with food and drink. And the man in the dirty coat had grabbed her, putting his filthy hand over her mouth. He'd been so strong and his hands so huge that she couldn't do anything. He'd dragged her through the woods to the hut. All she remembered was being tied up and gagged so she could hardly breathe. And he'd threatened her, kept calling her things like tarty girl and slut and slag and saying she was filthy. He kept saying how she'd pay for being such a slut. He hadn't done anything, other than threaten her, sometimes with a knife, sometimes with fire, sometimes with spiders. And he talked, crazy stuff about Nature's way and everything needing to be cleansed. Then Tom and I had turned up. That was all. She was shaking as she told me.

"Did you see a girl?" I asked, almost too scared to know.

"Where?"

"A girl who was with us."

"No, there wasn't a girl. Just you and Tom."

I called Mum and Dad back in. "It's OK," I said. "Laura will tell you now. And it's all right. Nothing happened."

No, nothing at all. Just that I'd lost the first girl I ever loved. And no one knew that I had lost anything at all.

Grandpa Apples

I went to stay with Grandpa for a few days after all. Home was weird just then. Full of confusion and emotions scraped raw and everyone being too careful. I thought I must be going mad. Crazy ideas grew in the greenhouse of my head, sprouting monstrous wings and faces that might be telling lies. In the wildest places of my brain I nurtured them and felt them taking over, spreading and choking all the tidy rows of reasonable thoughts.

But how could I say what was in my head? How could I ask dangerous questions like "Was this really all my fault?" or "Am I mad or evil?" And who would care that I had lost the girl whose name I still could not remember? Everyone was screwed up by what had happened, trying to heal themselves and each other, and there was no room for my frightening questions. It wasn't that they didn't try to help me—they did. In fact, they tried too hard. All the kindness and arms round my shoulders and the constant "We're so proud of you, Luke" just made everything worse.

But I went to stay with Grandpa on Grandpa-apple Wednesday. I felt floaty as I saw him waiting for our car at his front door, his smiling face and the smell of his home baking a warmed blanket.

We didn't talk about what had happened at first. I'd thought I would be bursting to talk, to sort it out, to find the answers, but I found that in his comfortable house, with all his souvenirs, everything just as it had been, my brain was soothed. Smoothed. Part of the great weight was being lifted and I felt that I could smile.

But Grandpa was not fooled. "Come and help me in the orchard, Luke. Let's take something to keep us going." And we each took a huge slab of his berry cake and some lemonade that had to be homemade. We walked together down to the orchard, the fresh morning breeze washing my head. Our job in the orchard was to clear the nettles and cut back the brambles, to make picking easier when the apples were ripe.

He came straight to the point as always, his clear blue eyes looking directly at mine, the pupils central and wise. Most people don't look directly at your eyes, but Grandpa does when he's saying something important.

"So, are you going to tell me all about it, Luke?" he asked.

"I don't know where to start," I said.

"Start at the beginning, of course," he said. "You don't have to tell me if you don't want to, you know? Your head is a secret place and you can keep some secrets there forever if you want to. But the trouble is that things in your head don't behave like real objects. They change and grow and sometimes, only sometimes, it's best to cut them out, like weeds in a garden. Like these nettles," and he smiled. "Come on, keep chopping—these nettles have got to go by suppertime."

I took the scythe—Grandpa was the only adult I knew who would let me use a scythe—and made a timid swipe at some nettles.

"Give it some welly, Luke!" I swiped harder. A huge swath of nettles lay neatly on the ground. Grandpa did the same and we attacked the nettles while I told him every-thing.

Everything about what happened in the woods, and about the girl, and Dreeg. My story, and what happened in the classroom. The pond, the poem, the newsletter. Flying. Laura. At the end I felt empty but terrified, terrified that Grandpa would not know what to say other than that I was bad or mad.

"Need the rakes now, Luke, and we'll get this lot cleared up."

"Well, what do you think? What was going on? Was it all my fault? Do you think I'm crazy?"

He leant on his rake and chewed a piece of grass.

"The mind's a funny thing. Plays tricks, you know? And the cleverest way the mind has of playing tricks is to take something that is as real as apples and then do things with it, change it in your mind. Some things were real, obviously. The man who took Laura—and that other girl before—he was real. And he did die in the fire, but that was his fault, and the best thing that could have happened, if you want my opinion. No messing around with trials and psychiatrists and people in newspapers going on about things they don't understand. What he did, what he was, that was nothing to do with your mind. And the fires, they happened anyway. Everyone knows that. And you rescued Laura. That took some courage—never forget that."

"Yes, but why was she there? Was it really because I wanted harm to come to her?"

"She was there because she was there. She went to the woods. The fact that you were angry with her has got absolutely nothing to do with what happened to her. It can't have. The world simply doesn't work like that, even if sometimes it seems to. That's where your mind played tricks. This Dreeg creature—figment of your imagination, a voice in your head. You were ill, Luke. Like hallucinating. Hey, but it must have been brilliant. That flying! What was it like?"

"Iced light. Lemon sherbet bursting on my tongue. The smell of frosted melon. The sound of strawberries. Don't know. I can't explain. It was like nothing in this world."

Grandpa's eyes shone. "But *I* know. I know exactly what you mean. When you said it, I knew exactly, for a second, what you meant. That's a skill, Luke, that's brilliant. That's a real power. Synesthesia, she called it. That's really something. And see? You still have it."

"Oh, I forgot to tell you one bit. You were in the story, Grandpa."

"Was I? What did I do?"

"You know the bit with the spiders?"

"Eugh. That was a scary bit."

"Well, I heard your voice. Just when I thought I was going to . . . die. You said, what was it? Something about 'Everything works out for the best in—' "

"The best of all possible worlds. Yes, I read it in a book. It's what I believe. Did I really say that in your story? Well, how about that, then!"

"And then you said, 'If you're not in it, you can't win it.' "

"How very wise I am." He chuckled. "What's it like to have a grandpa like me?"

It was pretty good, actually. Solid and real. Chocolate pudding. We finished our nettle-clearing and walked slowly back to the house with our tools. I noticed something. I noticed it as soon as I started walking.

My leg was getting better. The mist was lifting, drying up. Lightening. Just a little.

One more thing I had to ask. "What about that girl?" I asked Grandpa. "What was she?"

He stopped. "Let's be logical about this, Luke. No one else saw her. No one else spoke to her or noticed her at all as far as I can see. There was no girl in the woods, according to everyone who was there. She wasn't there, at least not in the real world. You made her in your head and she was just another figment of your imagination. They'd probably call it stress nowadays. The stress of being ill played tricks on you. She was nice to think about"—he winked—"but she wasn't real in the way you mean."

Even Grandpa isn't right about everything. I knew she had been real. If I could only remember her name, then I would know. It would make her real again.

As we reached the house, I said, "You know what you said? About being in it to win it? Well, will you help me?"

"Help you do what?"

"I want to run on sports day."

"Hmm. Don't know what your mother would say. Seems you've been doing a bit too much running recently."

"Oh, go on, Grandpa. It's just sports day. It's what I'm good at. And don't worry—I can run without winning."

Four days I stayed with Grandpa. He built me up like an athlete in training. He wrote out a plan and we went on the Internet and found out about the best food for athletes. I ran and walked and breathed and thought and rested. I did everything I was told. My leg wasn't completely better. There was no magic or anything. But it was good enough.

Sunday I went back home, leaving Grandpa smiling just as he had been when I arrived. And I was lighter, clearer, ready.

Laura was in the kitchen when I arrived home. Ladybirds in her hair. Her face clean.

"Want some cake?" she asked. And we sat and ate together. She looked pale as sugar, but her eyes were bright as they looked at me. Perhaps there was something dark in there, buried deep, but Grandpa told me that we have space in our brains to store some radioactive waste quite safely. Eventually it just loses all its poison. Part of growing up is learning that, he says. You grow away from it, start again, learn.

"You know what?" Laura said. "There's something I want to tell you." She paused. "You know that day when I read your poem?"

"Do you have to remind me?" What was this? Torture time? Payback?

"I saw her."

"What do you mean?" I breathed.

"You told me to read the poem out and I did. And when I read it I could see the girl you described. As though she was there. But I pretended not to. I wasn't going to admit that my kid brother could write something that brilliant. How did you do that?"

She didn't think I was nothing. The faraway taste of nursery music; soft mimosa singing; the sound of soap bubbles; a wave of warm hair. "I don't know. It was a fluke."

"But who is she?"

"She's no one. I made her up." And the smell of her now so faint I could barely hear it.

The Sound of Honey

Monday. **Mondays are red.** This still happens, you see. I do still have synesthesia, as the girl called it.

I could tell that Roach's patience was fraying. How much longer was he going to have to be nice to this boy who kept having the most absurd reasons for not doing his homework? Meningitis, fire, abducted sister, staying with his grandfather during term time—where would it end? But actually, I had finished the story in my own way at Grandpa's house and I gave it to him.

He read it in break time and spoke to me between lessons. "Brilliant, Luke. Most dramatic and creative. Perhaps a little over the top in places. I think perhaps I wouldn't have had spiders *and* fire. And the flying, I'm not really sure if that's believable, is it? But nevertheless, beautifully controlled and quite delightfully sinister." He was starting to sound like someone whose name I prefer not to mention.

"There's one thing you need to add, though. One answer which I think a reader would need."

"Oh?"

"The deaf girl. Who was she?"

"I don't really know. I just put that bit in because it seemed kind of good at the time but maybe she shouldn't be there. Maybe I should just take her out completely?"

"Well, it's nearly the end of term. You don't really want to be writing it out again, do you?" He laughed. "I'd just leave it if I were you. But well done, Luke. Excellent work. There's hope for you yet." And he wandered off alone to the staff room, his hands pushing his jacket pockets earthward. I put the story in the nearest bin. That's not to say I didn't think it was good—I did. I thought it was brilliant. But it was over. Time to move on.

Tuesday. Sports day.

I didn't win my race. I came second. In view of everything, I think that was good enough. Certainly from everyone's faces I knew it was good enough. Mum, Dad, Laura, Tom, Grandpa. From the sound of their cheering you would think I had won an Olympic medal. Mr. Breslin said, "Well done, Luke. A real fighter, you are. That's what we need. You have a good holiday, now. Get yourself rested. I'll see you next term."

I was happy with what I'd achieved without flying. I knew I would win next year. Felt it. No problems. And if I didn't, well, it wouldn't change the world.

After sports day was over I went to the woods with Amber. We walked through the devastation of the burnt trees. But already, some miraculous tiny shoots of green were poking through the ashes.

I found myself walking along the path toward the hut.

The sounds of birds grew quieter as we came near. I stood in the clearing and breathed it all in. The hut had been knocked down, perhaps by the firemen. I saw the tank of water, where I had wiped Laura's face. I saw the doorway where I had seen the mad old man with his one white eye and one blue. I stood among the wreckage and let it all pass through my head and out again for one last time.

What I was left with was the understanding that I had something to be grateful to Dreeg for: he had made me look inside myself and not like what I saw. However much of it was my fault, it didn't matter anymore because I had made it right in the end. And although I had lost something, how much more had I gained?

My eye caught something on the ground. I stooped down to pick it up. A drip of melted lilac. A twisted fingernail. Laura's, or—?

I left that place. But as I walked back across the clearing toward the path, with Amber scampering in the undergrowth nearby, I stopped again. I looked down at my feet for no reason that I could name. And there were tulips growing. Lilac tulips. The music of toasted cinnamon came to my lips and one word came swelling out from somewhere deep down inside me. *Seraphina.*

Seraphina. That was her name. And the real caramel smell of her washed over me as I looked up. She stood with her side to me some distance away, facing the clearing. Just standing silent, misty at the edges as though she might be a ghost. Musical notes floating in her hair. I couldn't move as I struggled to understand whether and why she was there.

If everything was over, if by flying again I had really lost all I had been offered and returned to normality, then why was Seraphina here? She was supposed to be a figment of my imagination—so Grandpa said.

I coughed, deliberately. She didn't hear. I called her name and she didn't blink. And so I walked until I was in front of her and smiled at her.

"Hello," I said, watching her reaction.

"Hello," she said, thickly through apple purée.

"How are you?" I said, which I know might seem rather odd, but it was all that came.

She laughed and as she did her head went back and three aquamarine butterflies flitted from her throat. One landed on my hand and shimmered there as it breathed in the biscuit air.

"Do I know you?" she asked.

Now, if this had been a corny film, I would have said in a husky voice, "No, but I know you." But as it was, I just said, "Luke, Patterson. I live round here."

"I've just moved here. My name is—"

"Seraphina," I interrupted. Couldn't help myself.

She laughed more butterflies. "What made you think that? It's Hannah. Just Hannah, nothing fancy."

But to me she would always be Seraphina, because she was the girl in my poem. The girl with the cinnamon skin, cake-warm, candy-floss bubbles on her breath, hair as long as the sound of honey.

Author's Note

To those of us who haven't experienced it, synesthesia seems a very strange condition. No one knows how many people have it, but there is a theory that all babies are born with it and that most lose it during the course of normal development.

No two people experience their synesthesia in exactly the same way. For some it simply means that when they think of a day of the week, they are bombarded with sensations of a particular color—and it will be the same color each time they think of that day. For others, life is a kaleidoscope of mixed sensations, where the noise of a train approaching will flood them with mesmerizingly detailed hues, and the noise of that same train screeching to a halt will stun them with quite different tastes, smells and colors, felt from the tips of their fingers to the very ends of their toes.

I don't have synesthesia but I know someone who does. For her it is the ordinary background to her life, a life that, it seems to me, must be richer than mine. What an advantage synesthesia would be for someone who wants to be a poet or artist, or to describe the world differently from the dull, expected version that most people see. I feel sure many artists and writers have synesthesia—perhaps it seems so ordinary to them that they haven't even noticed it.

The writer Vladimir Nabokov certainly had it and passed the condition to his son.

Think about high sounds and low sounds. Do the high sounds seem to have a brighter color and the low sounds a darker color? If so, you are touching on the world of synesthesia. Imagine, then, what it would be like if the sound of a violin produced the real taste of lemons in your mouth. . . .

One word of warning: people with synesthesia cannot fly, any more than the rest of us can. But they can open up the endless world of human imagination, and that, I believe, is the most amazing world of all.

N. M.

About the Author

I had a very odd childhood, although of course it seemed perfectly normal to me. I was born in a school, rather than a hospital, and I went to all-boys schools until I was eleven. I actually lived in the schools, which were surrounded by countryside, so in the holidays I had incredible freedom to roam about, on my pony, alone, inventing weird games of make-believe. The woods in *Mondays Are Red* are the woods where I galloped, and I can feel them now, years later. For me, they were the starting point for the book—everything else followed from there.

I've spent a long time trying to write a novel good enough to be published. At first, I always thought I would write for adults—I thought that was the only way I could use language in the way I wanted. But then, some years ago, I read David Almond's *Skellig* and I suddenly realized that powerful writing could be for everyone, not just adults. I'd like to think that *Mondays Are Red* is for everyone, or everyone who loves language.

I have always loved writing. I am fascinated by the effects of words—how choosing a slightly different word can conjure an entirely different spell. Language is much more important than mere communication—it's what makes humans different from other animals. Stories are important, but much more important to me is how the story is told. *Mondays Are Red* is about the power of language and power itself.

DATE DUE
REMINDER